The World Belongs to Jane & Me

(Part #1: 1963)

A TenGu Kru book

All rights reserved

This book is a work of fiction. While it makes reference to actual events and people, certain characters, characterisations, incidents, locations, products, and dialogue were fictionalised or invented for purposes of dramatization. With respect to such fictionalisation or invention, any similarity to the name or to the actual character or history of any person, living or dead, or any product or entity or actual incident is entirely for dramatic purposes and is not intended to reflect on any actual character, history, product, or entity.

No part of this book may be reproduced, or stored in a retrieval system, or transmitted in any form or by any means, electronic, mechanical, photocopying, recording, or otherwise, without express written permission of the publisher.

ISBN: 9798795795812
Imprint: Independently published
www.tengukru.bigcartel.com

Cover design by Adrian Stranik
Cover art by Gorki

Printed in England

To my father...
... and all the grunt 'n' groan gladiators of yesteryear.
I salute you.

CONTENTS...

Prologue	1
1) Carnage in Croydon	3
2) Westway Babylon	14
3) Shotgun	20
4) Over the River	35
5) Come Dancing	48
6) The Coffeeville Pinch	62
7) The Scrubs	68
8) Cinecittà Calling!	79
9) A Tale of Two Daddies	89
10) Kudos	109
11) Take Off	127
12) Boomerang Barb	138
13) Crossfire	150
14) Superhuman	168
15) Wild Weekend	183
Acknowledgements	194
About the author	198

"If you do this and God so commands, you will be able to stand the strain, and all these people will go home satisfied."

Exodus: 18:12

Your Opel Commodore pulls up hard with a chalkboard-scraping screech that contradicts its newness. That biting afternoon wind that comes in over Tooting Bec Common, and into this sedate Streatham suburb, does nothing to temper the hot violence you intend to exact as you propel yourself out of the car and up to those wide wrought-iron gates.

You try them.

They're locked.

You ignore the bell.

If there's an element of surprise to be had, you want it.

You jump the high stone wall and head up the gravel driveway to the big house. Lovely place. Mock Tudor. 1920s stained-glass window features and crawling with ivy.

Across the road, curtains twitch. Suburbia does what it does best—ignores crime and calls the police.

You peer through the letterbox but see no sign of life. The questionable need for a letterbox in an inaccessible door occurs as trivialities often do amid more crucial pursuits.

This pursuit being a reckoning that must surely conclude in bloodshed.

Someone is going to die.

Ten years ago, life was not *quite* so murderous . . .

HAMMERSTONE PROMOTIONS PRESENTS
INTERNATIONAL
ALL-IN WRESTLING SPECIAL

MAIN EVENT

KEN "VAMPYRE" WALKER
vs.
BOBI "HAMMERHEAD" OFEY

LONNIE & LINCOLN BORGE
(The Atomic Twins - direct from the USA)
vs.
TERRENCE "HOORAY" BUCKINGHAM &
CHARLIE '00' FLEMING
In a Tag Team Extravaganza!

KELLY HEWITT
vs.
THE DOMINATOR

DAMIEN LOGAN
vs.
NOEL POLEON "BONE-APART"

EVAN "HEAVEN" LEIGH
vs.
THE EGYPTIAN MAGICIAN

Tickets from Fairfield Halls Booking Office.
Telephone : CRO 9291

1963

1. CARNAGE IN CROYDON

The A23 cuts down through London's map like Al Capone's scar did down his face. It starts somewhere in Kennington and snakes its way south until it's engulfed, thirty miles later, by the Ringways death-race where holidays, hope, and estimations of making good time go to die.

But tonight, somewhere along that ancient road, we find ourselves at The Fairfield Halls: A two-thousand-seater in Croydon...

The building itself is an untroubled cliff face of brutalist concrete. Its few declarations of available wall space are plastered with multitudes of the same damp Letterpress poster—jammed frames of a demented telex machine—testifying to the tournaments within.

The night is wet and dismal. The kind of dismal only an April in Southwest London can manage. But it'll take more than lousy weather to keep these people home. The queue stretches around the block and winds slowly into the hall. A full house. Capacity exceeded. But still, in they come—3/6 for the cheap seats, all the way up to—10/6 ringside—a legion of overcoats and smouldering Embassy filters shuffle ever closer to the evening's salvation. It's here that the people will see TV stars in the flesh, battling it out for two falls or two submissions until one man holds dominion over another.

Last night it was *Rock and Roller*, Marty Wilde.

Tonight, it's the wrestling.

Proper wrestling.

'Cripple 'im!'

'Kill 'im, Kel!'

'Yeah, fuck him up!'

'Fuck 'im right up!'
'Get his mask off! Let's see him!'

This barb puts fire into the masked man who mangles his opponent's half-Nelson all to hell and lines him up for annihilation.

'It's all fixed though, innit? 'E hardly touched 'im!'
'G'wan, Kelleeeeeeeeeee!'

Hooded behemoth, the Dominator—a night-mare mass of a man—drop-kicks Kelly Hewitt with a hard smack in the bare chest that bounces him off the corner like a pinball.

This is more like it.

They want to feel it, this power, and they feel it now.

The crowd roars thunderously.

Millions watch it on the box, so they have to water it down for the telly—for the young and old 'uns, you understand.

Blood drawn on a prime-time Saturday afternoon?!

Not on your Nellie.

They'd take it off before you could say *Tessie O'Shea*.

But tonight . . . out here . . . in the suburbs . . . away from the cameras . . .

The vast expanse above the heaving crowd is loaded with fag clouds and sweltering humidity.

Inhale to your heart's content! the advert commands us.

'Do 'im, D!'
'Yeah, fuck him up!'

It's been decided.

The Dominator to win. Kelly Hewitt is dischuffed.

But fuck him.

He'll do as he's told.

Yeah, *he'll* do as he's told.

He'll take the fall alright.

But *his* way.

'What's the difference between Mandy Rice-Davies and the Eiffel Tower?'

The Egyptian Magician knows mirth is imminent and plays along. 'Go on.'

Evan delivers. 'Not everyone's been up the Eiffel Tower.'

The crowded dressing room heaves with fighters in various stages of undress. The sweltering air chokes on itself—on the musk of jangling testosterone and cheap 'paint-stripper' aftershave. Brut, Old Spice, Tabu . . . Not so much the smell of men as the scent of 20th century advertisement aspiration—the funk of urban gladiators who tonight will ascend mountains of an inner-city Asgard. Pecs and abs flex and un-flex—poses aplenty, in front of stand-up mirrors for the benefit of their peers. These specimens run the gamut of manhood. You've got the pretty boys—the dazzlers—preening, immaculate examples of physical perfection. Then there's the old school—the heavy-duty grapplers, cauliflower ears and bowlegged, from twenty years of armlocks, full-nelsons and Boston crabs. And then there's the run-to-fat slobs; moonlighting lorry drivers here to impress their birds. You usually put them on early while the people are still finding their seats.

Evan "Heaven" Leigh and Kareem "The Egyptian Magician" Rizk sit on a bench over by the wall, balls-out naked but for their unlaced boots, reading the papers. The headlines carry the latest updates on the Profumo scandal. The Secretary of State for War has been caught with his weapon in a couple of cookie jars by the names of Christine Keeler and Mandy Rice-Davis.

'Pair of little scrubbers' surmises the Magician.

The Egyptian Magician is not from Egypt. He's from Dagenham. But, in this world, the wrestling world, his swarthy appearance dictates that he is foreign and, therefore, in this case, Egyptian. When he enters the ring, he wears the Fez. So the throngs of grunt 'n' groan fanatics are under no illusions: the *Magician* has just flown in from North Africa for the sole purpose of threatening English sensibilities. The people thrive on hard lines. They like to know who their enemies are.

Fez + Swarthy = Enemy.

Evan is a piss-taker—a wind-up merchant—the class clown. With Evan, a good laugh is never more than a one-liner away. His angelic blue eyes dance and twinkle before he delivers one of his jests or putdowns.

If you're black. You're a black cunt.

If you're fat. You're a fat cunt.

If you've got a big nose. Big nose cunt.

Glasses? Four-eyed cunt.

The rest of us, using Evan's loose designations?

We're just cunts.

The black 'head-butt specialist' Bobi "Hammerhead" Ofey saunters past on the way to the shitter. Evan assails him with his Mandy-Rice Davis joke.

Bobi enjoys Evan's mirth, as do all the boys. Bobi's guttural, subterranean chuckle could be from the pistons of a midnight steam train.

Out in the vast hall, the one men call the Dominator delivers skull cracking forearm smashes to Kelly Hewitt's pulpy head that can be felt up in the bleachers.

The assault sends him sailing through the ropes like a thrown shovel. The man doesn't even try to protect himself. He hits the concrete, face down, like a slab of meat. He rises with badge-of-honour grit stuck in his face. The roar of the crowd is a vindication, a baptism of his agony. Hewitt's pain-threshold is something to behold—something to revile. He staggers comically, his thick strawberry blonde mop obscures his bloodied face. He absorbs the crowds' noisy approval. It recharges him. He turns on his heel, flicks his hair back and climbs up into the ring for a final reckoning with the Dominator who prowls the apron, throwing fuck-you fists to the mob.

The two men charge and lock arms, brutality incarnate. The Dominator might be old, but he's no pushover. But then

Hewitt is a grade-A nutcase of Bedlam proportions. The kind of bloke they wouldn't put in the army for being too berserker, even for them. For Hewitt, pain is an exotic wonder—a fascinating toy to be played with and tested—as a troubled child might torment a small animal. Only, Hewitt *is* the child *and* the animal, and the symbiosis gets off in a self-perpetuating vortex of sensation.

But now, Hewitt is tired of playing with himself and toying with his opponent.

Clown-time is over.

Now it's time to dominate the Dominator . . .

Three miles north, at that very moment, along that A23—at Leigham Court Road, Streatham to be precise—Jonny 'The Kid' Arnold and 'Flash' Nicky Nash are waiting under the awning, out of the rain. The big clock jutting out of the South London Press building across the road, five floors above them, says twenty to nine.

Nicky compares the clock to his Rolex and sees the exquisite timepiece is a couple of minutes shy. Gary 'the nose-biter' appears in his mind's eye—the man he bought it from—and wonders if he's been sold a dud. Or worse, a fake. He'll have one of his Jew chums have a gander. Give it the once over. If it turns out not to be kosher, Gary will be getting a visit—fearsome rep or no fearsome rep. When someone takes the piss, news travels fast. As does correct and proper resolution. Such are the rules of Nicky's game. Rules that are about to be applied tonight . . . to Harold 'Spider' Webb and Sammy Fortnoy.

No-one intends this to be the works.

No.

Nicky and Jonny 'The Kid' are here to stay the course of propriety. Of course, things *could* get silly. Harold and Sammy *could* give them some static and then they might have to be taken in hand. Putting some knuckle about can go a long way to maintaining the SQ.

As is often the case, Nicky's on a windup. '*Wrestlers* . . . they're all puppy squeezers. Y'know that, dontcha?'

Jonny won't entertain it. 'If he's not here in five minutes, we're going. We're late as it is.'

'It's no job for a bloke, anyway . . . leaping around in your pants . . .' The words bustle their way around the hot sausage roll Nicky is munching, ' . . . you gotta be a fucking queer to wanna do that.'

Jonny has heard it all before. He sidesteps the diatribe. 'You sound like my old man.'

Always in black is Nicky. The three-button jacket; drainpiped trousers; winkle-picker boots; hair oiled, quiffed and duck-arsed . . . If it weren't for the Saville Row-grade white shirt disrupting the darkness, he'd look like an undertaker. Thick black horn-rimmed glasses sit across a prominent, somewhat regal nose. Wiry, tall but toned. At twenty-nine years old, Nicky is a leftover 1950s "angry *not-so-young* man". The 60s are yet to find him. But then, the 60s are yet to find any of us. The Beatles are still just another noise from up north and the American president's head is yet to be torn apart by Soviet bullets. But, for all his wide-boy bluster, there's something Zen and all-knowing about Nicky Nash, and by the same token he's as much a thug as the lunatics he runs with.

He looks after himself, but to Jonny, in all that black, Nicky Nash looks like an arrangement of liquorice.

Jonny Arnold - AKA Kid "Tarzan" Jonathan - is a springloaded walking erection. Nineteen years old, just five, seven tall, Tony Curtis hair, blackened with Brylcreem, all carried by a frame sculptured by seven years of bench presses, curls, pull-ups, press-ups—the result of thirty-thousand odd gym hours. His fists might be small, but they're all the more devastating for it. A lot of power focused in a small area amounts to devastation for their receivers. His black Joe Weider T-shirt shows off the tats on his forearms. The shirt might not tell the world who he is—but, as the rain tightens it to his formidable chest, it tells *him* who he is. The world will know in due course.

Tonight, the boys are on a search and destroy.

Search for Samuel Fortnoy.

Tell him what's what.

Destroy him if he fails to comply.

This is Nicky's deal.

Jonny is here to amplify the point, should one need to be amplified. He's a known toughy, so his presence is usually enough to encourage the natural order of things. He's not interested in slapping errant pornographers around. He's only here for the score—the twenty quid that Nicky gives him for these gigs.

It continues to piss down, so they wait in the doorway of this high-end flat block. Gangsters live here. Richardson's lot mainly: the torture squad. Or, at least, this is where they install their bits on the side to crash with when trying to dodge their wives.

Nicky knows most of them, the *chaps, and* their bits on the side. *Especially* their bits on the side. A few of "the boys" know their girls feature in his blue films and don't mind at all. You might be surprised at how many of their girlies go for the idea—drop their drawers as soon as you start waving a camera about. But most *don't* know what their girls get up to. So skilfully choreographed subterfuge is the order of Nicky's days. And he does it very well . . .

Action.

Across the road an 'Opalescent Maroon' Jag pulls up. Two men get out and approach the building.

They're suited.

Booted.

As all of "Rich" Clifford Sherman's boys are.

They're bickering over something and haven't seen Nicky and Jonny haunting the shadows. Nicky spits a half-chewed piece of sausage roll into his palm. 'Watch this.'

As the two men reach the pavement, Nicky throws the piece of food. With incredible accuracy, the missile hits the back of Sammy's throat. He staggers back into the road, choking on the unwelcome surprise. A speeding car swerves to avoid him and honks angrily.

Nicky and the Kid close in.

Jonny points right at Spider, 'Keep walking!'

'What?!'

'Keep walking. Don't look back. Don't you *fucking* look back!'

Jonny kicks Spider hard up the arse. He squeals and runs off down to the high street.

Nicky drags Sammy onto the pavement by his tie and slaps him across the face. 'Nothing'll fuck you quicker than a big mouth, Sammy! Tomorrow! The Dorchester! Twelve! You've got some ironing to do!'

Jonny watches Spider disappear around the corner and calls to Nicky, 'C'mon, the show's gonna be over before we get there.'

They drive off, leaving Samuel Fortnoy kneeling in the flooded gutter, coughing up Nicky's second-hand sausage roll.

Hewitt ducks down and feigns a clumsy grab for behind the Dominator's knees. On instinct, the Dominator bends over Hewitt's back, locking his arms around Hewitt's waist and holds his head between his legs. Hewitt straightens up, with the Dominator now holding on to his back, upside down, with a face full of Hewitt's arse. This is Hewitt's signature move—the double-elbows drop. Hewitt throws himself high and backwards, sending both men up and over in a skyward and spectacular arc. The impact of the Dominator hitting the canvas with all of Hewitt's 220 pounds on top of him can be seismically registered in Surbiton. The masked man's lungs seize. The subways of his aorta judder to a stop.

The crowd screams blue murder. The old bags are out of their seats and lay siege to the ring, wielding sharp brollies and vicious intent. Screeching harpies are these.

Hammerstone's head honcho, Jock Hammer, clocks it first. The Dominator's exposed arms and legs take on a blueish hue.

Jock yells to the MC—at the bucket boys standing ringside, 'He's hurt! Turn the fucking lights on!'

The crew are on their feet and absorb the spectacle of the prone man, bathed in an anodyne yellow glow that casts the blue gloom out. The crowd rises and takes a calming, collective drag on their fags, craning their necks for a better view. They murmur casual concern. They whisper satiated fears. Others are still yelling, oblivious to the cessation of action.

Referee Reg has seen dodgy falls before, and this looks just like one. At Hewitt, he screams, 'What have you done now?! *You fucking nutter*!'

The question and its answer fall on nonchalant ears. Reg disengages himself from his useless rebuke and attends the fallen man.

Hewitt does that head toss thing again, flinging his long thin hair back—the sweat-sodden remnants of a joke-shop fright-wig.

The crowd emerges from a collective fit, like an abducted nation freed from an alien dimension. Awe and embarrassment dilute the angry air. The nicotine fog renders the scene a fading dream. The crew—the ring rats—leap into the ring and surround Reg and the unconscious masked man.

Confusion rots into panic and tightens its dreadful squeeze. A bucket boy leaps out over the ropes and runs for the foyer phone.

Gil Stone, Jock's brother-in-law and Hammerstone's second-in-command, nudges Reg aside and attends the fallen man himself. Straight away, he sees that the

Dominator needs what he doesn't have. 'Is there a doctor in the house?!'

Reg reiterates, louder, '*Is there a doctor in the house*?!'

Hewitt patrols the apron of the ring, mid-preen, and wonders where his adulation went.

It's all fixed though, innit?

Nicky's Ford Zodiac pulls up across the road from the Fairfield Hall. Jonny grabs his holdall off the back seat and pushes against the tide of the crowd who are spilling out of the venue and on to the street. Nicky parks the car and saunters across the puddle-dashed road after him.

A St. John's ambulance crew is here now. Inside, those wrestlers, the preening dazzlers and the fat slobs alike, mill around en masse, robed and half-dressed, watch as the Dominator, still in his black mask, is lifted out of the ring and onto a stretcher. Seems wrong somehow, to expose him in his time of defeat.

Geoff the M.C comforts Charlie "00" Fleming, who sobs into a towel. 'That's it, I'm done. I'm never fighting again!'

Geoff hugs him. 'C'mon, Charlie. He'll be okay. He'll be okay...'

Jock and Gil assess broken Charlie. 'Geoff,' Jock says to the MC. 'Get him home. I'm going to the hospital with Dom.'

The architect of all this heartbreak is nowhere to be seen. Kelly Hewitt is probably halfway up that A23 by now, on his way back to his Yorkshire pig farm, oblivious to the chaos in his rear-view.

Jonny enters the hall with Nicky right behind him. Crew humpers are dismantling the ring.

Jonny goes over there; to Evan, who he "sort of" knows. 'What happened?'

'It's Dom,' Evan answers vacantly. This situation is beyond humorous possibilities, so he's in unfamiliar territory. 'He took a bad fall. Hewitt done it'

Desperately, Jonny scans the room for signs of salvation—anything that might get his pursuit back on track.

Nicky goes over to Gil. 'I brought Jonny the Kid.'

Gil is all distraction. Naturally, given the circumstances.

But part of him is present enough to ask, 'Who?'

'*Jonny the Kid.* Jonny Arnold.' Nicky tilts his head in the Jonny's direction. Jonny stands there, expectant. Eager. Failing to read the room. 'You *know*, Kid "Tarzan" Jonathan.'

Gil glances over at the agitated young man and reiterates, 'Never 'eard of 'im.'

'The Kid. *The Kid.* He's fucking great. I told you I was gonna bring him tonight. You said bring him. So here he is.'

Gil remains distracted. A state he will occupy for some time. 'Not tonight, Nicky. Bring him round tomorrow, yeah? Tomorrow.'

2. WESTWAY BABYLON

Within the hour, Nicky drops Jonny at Victoria station.

'This alright?'

The question draws Jonny out of his reverie. 'Yeah. I can get a 52 from here.'

'You still living in Notting Hill?'

'Notting *Dale*.'

'Oh, Lovely.'

Jonny gets out and stands there with his holdall.

Nicky winds down his window. 'You gonna be alright, yeah?'

'Yeah.'

'Dom is a fat fuck, Jonny. He should never have been in the ring in the first place. Those old fuckers make a name for themselves back in the forties or whatever—twenty years later they're still a draw and they milk it—*bound* to come unstuck eventually. He'll be alright, anyway. He's old school. Tough.'

Jonny waits for Nicky to move the car so he can cross the road to the bus stop.

'We'll go over tomorrow if you want', Nicky says, cheerfully. 'I'm in Brixton, anyway.'

'Brixton?'

'Yeah, their head office.'

'They got a head office?'

'Yeah, we just went past it.'

'Can't. I'm getting married tomorrow.'

'Married! Seriously?'

'Yeah, getting married.'

'Who's the lucky bird?'

'You don't know her.'

Nicky is dubious. He knows a lot of birds. 'Bring her out sometime. I'll bring my missus.'

'Yeah, alright.'

The car pulls away and disappears into Friday night traffic. The drizzle eases off some. Jonny watches two tramps rummage through dustbins outside the Palace Theatre, pulled-up collars on their greasy tweed coats.

Some of the cast of the Black and White Minstrel show, sans greasepaint, exit the theatre's glass doors in a bustle of post-show high spirits and sore throat hilarity.

A copper approaches and moves the tramps on. 'Get along there, you!'

The 52 is early...

The bus ride is a slow-moving trance—a stop/start parade of neon break-lights and rain-smashed pavements—warm lights from the interiors of homely flats over closed shops. Going west...

Tonight should have been the night. The night it would all happen... The head honchos at Hammerstone Promotions would get a load of Jonny and sign him up on the spot. They had a head office in Brixton? Jonny imagined they were a transient always-on-the-move tribe that landed where they would. *Coming to an arena near you!*

Five years, he's been down here. Got his first proper match three years ago. Thought it was a simple matter of a television talent scout seeing you, recognising your brilliance and signing you up for the telly.

That's how it works, right?

Wrong.

A chance comment from Nicky the other day outlined the brutal truth. All the TV stars worked for Hammerstone Promotions and Hammerstone Promotions *only*! If you wanted to make it—*really* make it—then they were the portal through which stardom awaited. If you weren't on the telly, you didn't exist. And they didn't come to you. You had to go to them. And Nicky knew 'em all.

It's not *what* you know...

Notting Dale.

   A valley of dens.

   Drinking dens.

   Gambling dens.

   Knocking shops.

   And begrudgingly squeezed between them ... the bedsits.

   People have to sleep sometime.

   Somewhere ...

Jonny hits the switch. The bulb flickers and protests ... flickers and protests ... until the feeble current has its way. Twelve feet by sixteen of damp, broken plaster and bare splintering floorboards. The kind of hole the word dismal was made for. He nearly trips over the plate of sandwiches the landlady left on the floor for him.

He drops his bag on the wooden chair. The chair doubles—actually *triples*—as a seat, a coat hanger and bedside table. The small stove in the corner was a remnant of the Boer War, according to Stefania, the landlady. He lifts the tinfoil off the plate. Corn beef and pickle. Fucking angel, that bird. If she was born this century, he'd show her his appreciation. He drops himself on the narrow prison bunk and munches big. Whatever he lost of himself tonight is partially replaced with this meal.

The wall before him is awash with pages, carefully removed from American wrestling magazines. Modern-day gladiators; 'Nature Boy' Buddy Rogers; Don Leo Jonathan; Crazy Luke Graham; Johnny Valentine; Dick the Bruiser; Dr. Jerry Graham ... The Yanks. They know how to put on a show.

Of course, he'd never seen these men in the flesh, but you could see the poetry of them. Their stances transcend the hopeless static of these rough photographs and leapt off the page.

   Mythological creatures from a land, far ... far away ...

   Jonny will join their pantheon one day.

   And yet ...

Married tomorrow . . .

Jonny had to wonder if it was a sheer lack of balls that put him here instead of a big county pile somewhere, and not just lousy luck.

He'd been fixed.

Zen.

On-target.

Tonight was meant to be his intro to the big boys at Hammerstone's. *Britain's premier wresting promotions!*

So much for turning his life around.

With what he made at that Acton nut and bolt factory and the odd match for the independents, he could barely feed and clothe himself, let alone a wife with one on the way. When she came out of that clinic with a smile on her face, he thought they'd dodged a bullet.

Seventeen.

She didn't need this shit either.

Her nervous smile broke and disintegrated into a hot flood of tears. All the worry of the two weeks previous solidified into panic and fear. He'd not seen that on a girl's face before. That kind of fear. His own fear of seeing that compelled him to blurt out, 'We better get married then.'

Five years, he's been down here. Since the summer of '58. Just in time to miss Buddy Holly at the Gaumont, but not the riots in Notting Hill Gate. They invited him—those Teds—to *beat up wogs* in Keslake Road. Jonny seldom had a problem with the darkies. Never even met one until he came down here and got to know a few at the gym. There'd be the odd skirmish, but then, Jonny had odd skirmishes with all sorts of people. On average, they were friendlier than most of the Londoners he'd encountered. Up to a point, he shared their outsider status. So yeah, he accepted the Teds' invite.

A noisy house party in the front garden of number 57. The Teds made the charge. Leapt over the low wall and got busy with the clubs and razors. Jonny brought up the rear—brick in each hand—and cracked every duck's arse he saw.

The upside: word got around, and Jonny never had a problem with the blacks in that neck of the woods from that day on. Even got invited to a few of those blues parties they were always having.

Only ever went to one.

Liked the music.

Loved the food!

Some of them birds didn't fuck about, neither.

But couldn't stand the smoke.

Fuck, they liked to smoke.

The downside?

He had to duck and dodge those fucking Teds from that day onward ... He used to be one himself—a Teddy Boy—back in Brynmawr. But after that Keslake tear up, he hung up his drape-coat, never to be worn again. His peacock days were over. For now.

Married in the morning ...

Time for a recap.

A re-think.

Tonight's setback will not prevent the inevitable.

He takes the bottle of milk from off the outside window-ledge and gulps half of it in one go.

In the distance there is yelling and the sound of breaking glass. At the end of the alley, he sees a couple of blacks run past ... a gang of Irish in hot pursuit ...

The woman in the window opposite is doing her usual routine—parading around her living room with her tits out, pretending she isn't being watched. He has to wonder if this show was for him alone or is there a whole wall of spectators around the neighbourhood, dick in hand, racing to the finish before she pulls her blinds? She does so now, so he's missed the show.

Just as well.

Married tomorrow.

Better get used to the focus—to the one-woman-man shtick.

Is it even possible?

To only want one woman?

It's kind of against nature, ain't it?

He checks his reflection in the mirror, flexing his chest and arms, studying them from every conceivable angle. He sits on the edge of the bed, picks weights up from the floor and does a few 100-pound curls.

The day has not been what it should have been. It should have been a new beginning.

Tomorrow will be another—a new beginning. But not the *right* beginning.

He should be up there on that wall, with Don Leo Jonathan and the rest, looking down on himself now.

Not down here looking up.

Not getting married in the morning . . .

3. SHOTGUN

The alarm goes off at five minutes to nine. It rings and jangles until his arm—also jangling with pins and needles—can snake out and grasp around for the travel clock under the chair.

He puts the kettle on and makes porridge. Breakfast of a would-be champion. The wedding is at three. He has to pick up the suit from the cleaners on Latimer Road and re-sole the only proper shoes he has with the inside of a cornflakes packet. Has to buy some cornflakes first—doesn't want to break the score Nicky gave him for a packet of cornflakes—so needs to see what spare change is in the tin.

'I left sandviches for you. You get 'zem?'

Stefania, the landlady, speaks through the gap in the door. He always leaves it ajar once he's up because he knows she likes a chat and wants her to know she is always welcome to do so. Ultimately, it's her place, so she can do whatever the fuck she likes. But the woman operates within the bounds of a mutually understood propriety which gives this old Czech carte blanche as far as he's concerned. Plus, the sandwiches loomed legendary, so largess begat largess.

'I got 'em Stef, and they were fucking lovely.'

She accepts this as the welcome it is and comes in wrapped in a thick, woollen night coat. 'My godt, you are not eefen dressed! Vot time iss it, ze vedding?'

Jonny eats his thin porridge at the window in his Weider T-shirt and Y-fronts, and wonders what 'tits' over the way is doing behind her blinds. Is Stefania aware of the local entertainment?

'I got hours. It's not 'til three.' He holds up the tin bowl. 'Porridge. Want some?'

'Sat vatery rubbish you eat? I'd rasser drink piss.'

Jonny splutters on it and spits it out through the open window. 'It's all I can afford!'

'Vot you do, you young boyss?' Steering to the matter at hand. 'You get zem in tvouble and now you haff to marry zem? Zo crazy.'

He felt himself adopted. The woman had no man about the house, spoke of no children. He knew she was Czechoslovakian but couldn't remember how he knew this. Maybe she had mentioned it while his mind was elsewhere, as it often was. Or, maybe, he'd seen her letters from the old country, post-marked accordingly. *Kuntova* was her surname. You had to laugh. They were on opposite ends of the human spectrum. She, an old woman. He, a young man. But both exiles in their way. Of course, neither of them featured on the bottom rung—on the sign that hung on many a local establishment—*No blacks. No Irish. No dogs.* He was sure that if this list contained a fourth entry, it would include the Welsh. But then, when they said *Irish*, they probably meant anyone that wasn't English. Ancient beefs rang eternal.

'You luff ziss girl?'

'Wha' he spluttered again, 'What?!'

'Zimple qvestion. Do you? Luff har?'

'I don't know. Yeah. We're gettin' married, ain't we?'

She shrugs. 'I zink maybe you put ze horse before zee cart. Maybe if you two rilly haff sumzing you vill find it later. You should hope you know it vhen it comes. You don't vont to miss sumsing.'

He flings the remnants of the porridge from the bowl through the window and watches with satisfaction as it splashes on the cobblestones below. A black cat dodges it then comes back to investigate with jerky, tentative movements of his head.

Somewhere in the distance, an ambulance bell is ringing. Jonny has emergencies of his own. He gets dressed while the woman watches, grabs his jacket off the back of the chair. She squeezes his dick as he brushes past her. She always does this. Maybe it's a Czech thing. Maybe she just likes to cop a feel—dirty old cow. No harm done, right?

'Back in an hour.'

Fucking balls!

Nattering with the landlady has caused Jonny to forget the twenty quid note Nicky gave him and leave it in his other trousers. And now Mr George wants to play hardball, and all Jonny has is the change in his jacket. He's sixpence shy, and this big Greek prick isn't going to do him any favours. He thinks he can see the suit there, under its paper cover, hanging up in the back.

'Give me a fucking break. It's for a wedding. *Mine*. I'm getting married today.'

'Third one.'

'What?'

'I said thiiiiird one! You third one today, say it's for wedding.'

'Well, maybe there's a lot of love in the air. Come on, don't be a cunt. You know me! You know I'm good for it.'

'I no know you! I have trusted customer list. You're not on it. I have only one Mr Arnold and he's dead. Last week. Fell in canal. Tangled in tugboat. Very nasty.'

Two old biddies clatter and clang in through the door.

'You know price. Can't let suit go without it.' Mr George reiterates, 'It's bad business . . . bad business,' and goes over to attend the women.

Jonny assesses the ladies and the likelihood of their philanthropy. Their coats are threadbare, and their shoes have been shuffling up and down Ladbroke Grove since Hitler put that gun in his mouth.

Then he sees her.

Through the window across the road, coming out of Woolworths, in a blue coat: his betrothed.

Jane Porter.

She has a way of being above the crowd even as she walks among it, head held high, like she is focused on something that she has to get to at the end of the street. Whatever she sees has her whole attention and nothing, seemingly, can divert her from it. For outsiders, this raw neighbourhood is a world to be feared. But this is her manor. This is her world in a way that it will never be Jonny's.

The unnecessary saviour within compels him to come out of the shop, into this bright and hopeful morning, but he hesitates at the kerb. He wants to watch her, disconnected from him. It's like seeing her for the first time. And in a way, it is. His entire experience of her was when they were together—Jonny & Jane. Jane Porter is a thing to behold. She is back to being the exciting stranger she was in the moment before he met her, standing with a friend outside her family's block of flats at Octavia House, smoking cigarettes. Her chocolate brown hair tied back in a ponytail. Pale pink lipstick coated full, sensuous lips: cheekbones, high and sharp. Her friend, Maureen, was a looker too, like a skinny Diana Dors, but Jane, in her brown and cream woollen twinset with gold buttons, was a cut above. He could see it a mile off. He hated cigarettes—especially girls smoking them—but take the fags away and she could be Jane to his Tarzan. They could *rule* this fucking jungle. When he found out her name *was* Jane, it seemed like a sign. When he found out that her surname was Porter, just like in the Edgar Rice Burroughs books, it sealed the deal.

He had no doubts that he could get this coffee-bar teenage queenie to forsake nicotine for a Welsh Adonis with sure-fire glory emblazoned in his stars.

And that's how it started.

She told him she was a virgin.

And so was he, virtually.

He'd had his first jump just before he left home, with the daughter of one of his father's God-bothering brethren from their local chapel. Jonny's prayers had at last been answered that night, but God moves in annoying ways and had only answered them three times since, with a couple of the girls and a frustrated housewife from the Acton nut and bolt factory he did the odd job for. Then he met her, the girl from Octavia House.

It had been the friend, Maureen, who was all over him. Jane observed Maureen's manoeuvres that frosty December day outside the flats with seemingly detached bemusement. Jonny was to learn that Maureen was very . . . *very* . . . engaged and Jane knew her friend would never have been able to make good on her promise to meet Jonny the following night at the Odeon to see Kirk Douglas in *The Vikings*. Maureen's fiancé was a violently jealous Geordie whose powers of surveillance would impress the KGB. Her movements were meticulously kept track of. So, it was Jane who turned up at the cinema that night, and it was *she* who shared those frantic bus-stop feel-ups, those soaring alleyway hand-jobs, and that searing sealed-the-deal afternoon when her family were out, when they finally shared a bed, resulting in that world-shattering visit to the clinic, six weeks later. So much for that fucking pill they're all on about. Where do you even get it?

Only they and her folks knew that human history is about to change ever so slightly. He also knows that she might have the sixpence he needs to get his suit out of the dry cleaners.

She sees him standing there across the busy high street.

On sight of each other, they freeze.

Fuck it.

He goes over and she looks down at the points of her shoes, at their proximity to the edge of the gutter.

She seems to be talking to her shoes when she says, 'They reckon it's bad luck to see each other on the day of your wedding.'

'Hopefully, we've had all our bad luck.'

'Hopefully.' Finally, she looks at him. 'You look rough. Stag night?'

'*Stag night*? Who'd I have a stag night with?'

'I dunno. Mates?'

'What mates?! No, I was over in Croydon trying to get a match. One of the wrestlers got hurt, and they stopped the show. So couldn't see the head honchos. So, now I've got to go all the way over there again to where they're based in Brixton.'

'Thought you'd be in the Western, gettin' smashed.'

'The Western? Fuck that. Your old man drinks in there.'

'So, what you doin' 'ere then?'

'I'm trying to get my suit out of that fucking laundry place.'

She looks over at the blue and white edifice of Georgios' Dry Cleaners. 'What's stopping you?'

'I'm sixpence short. Prick won't budge.'

She opens her purse and hands him the tiny silver coin.

He puts it in a pocket, quick. The embarrassment is mutual.

He sees the paper bag in her hand. 'Whatcha get?'

'Lipstick.'

'Pink?'

'Yeah.'

He has to laugh, so he does. In a quick yuk.

The subsequent pause is awkward. She puts it out of its misery. 'We don't *have* to do this, you know. *You* don't have to do this.'

'There's no way around it. Anyway, I want to.'

She's not convinced. She looks up the street. There's nothing convincing there either. She locks his steely blues with her sapphires. 'See you at the altar, then.'

She walks away.

He watches her.

She looks good.

It could be worse.

He shouts after her. 'Well, what do *you* want?'

She shouts back—over the growl of a passing bus. He can barely hear her. But it sounds like . . . 'It don't matter what I *want*, I love ya!'

If this was a movie, the do-woppy *When We Get Married* by The Dreamlovers would be playing over this scene. But it isn't. So, the rumble of Harrow Road's heavy traffic and the photographer, moonlighting from his usual local press gig, shouting directions, will have to do.

Mr Jonathan and the newly appointed Mrs Jane Arnold stand as one on the steps of the old Registry Office. The service was brief and clinical. Devoid of whatever sentiment you'd associate with a public declaration of love, honour and . . . whatever the last one is. A small group of Jane's family and friends flank the awkward couple. Maureen is there with her jealous Geordie, Jane's mum and dad, Carol and Harold, her nine-year-old sister Connie in bridesmaid's apparel, and be-suited brothers, David, (The oldest, an overgrown Ted of the stripe that ran with those idiots over Kensal Rise) and fourteen-year-old Danny: the only one of Jane's family that Jonny actually likes—*The birdman of Octavia House*—loves animals and nature as much as Jonny does.

Jane looks an absolute doll in the creamy dress her mother made, and Jonny can't take his eyes off her. Yeah. It could be worse.

The photographer positions everybody for the next picture.

'Okay, and . . . cheeeeeeeeeeeeeeeeeeese!'

They all say, 'Cheeeeeeeeeeeeeeeeeeeeeeeese!'

A gritty high street wind whips away fluttering confetti.

The groom whispers to his bride, 'My mother is gonna fucking strangle me when she finds out.'

The reception is in an upstairs room of the Eagle pub on the corner of Middle Row, just across the road from the Forester's Wrestling Club. The club's proximity lends Jonny the doggedness he didn't know he needed to get through this day.

Using a sizable chunk of that twenty quid Nicky gave him for last night's Sammy and Spider thing, Jonny was able to book a room here for the wedding night. Jane's lot forked out for this function room and did the food: cucumber and salmon sandwiches and cheese and pineapple chunks on cocktail sticks.

Danny plays records on the dancette he brought over: Guy Mitchell . . . Jonnie Ray . . . Frankie Laine . . . but Tommy Steele, mainly. Their mum loves Tommy Steele. Jane loved Tommy too until Elvis happened.

Forlornly, Jonny watches stranger after stranger come in and zero in on people they know. The party grows with the addition of those who were not at the ceremony itself, but already ensconced in this antiquated boozer. The men in their oversized suits seem vacant and defeated until the drink does its work. Now they're all backslapping bonhomie and dirty jokes. There will be punch-ups later. It wouldn't be a wedding without one—and Jonny tries to guess which of them would be the instigators. None convey hostility . . . *yet*.

The women over a certain age are, for the most part, over-painted, misshapen hags. The younger ones, probably their daughters, are fast heading for the same fate. Jonny gives them half a decade and wonders at why people would let themselves go like that.

Jane's dad is downstairs in the bar with her brother David and their power-station workmates, which suits Jonny just fine.

Paulie Ingram is a no-show. Jonny hoped his old schoolmate would bring the moral support he would never admit he could do with. It was Paulie who got him hooked on the wrestling in the first place.

'You ever seen a wrestling match, Jonny? I'm goin' with my dad. Wanna come?'

Wrestlers featured heavily in the bodybuilding magazines Jonny devoured as a kid, so it was off to Stowe Hill Baths Hall in Newport that the excited trio went to see the fearsome Bert Assirati against Vic Hessle.

Now *that* was a tear up!

Vic was wrestling royalty and had been a force to be reckoned with since the 30s. But Bert Assirati? Your force had to be supernatural to face that fucker down.

Bert had a head like a bullet, a neck like a bull, huge shoulders, massive arms, a sixty-inch chest, a thick but hard looking waist and hips set on two short tree-trunk legs. The man was only about 5' 6" tall but weighed around 270 pounds. Imagine a hairless gorilla with shorter arms. That would be Bert.

Early in the fight, Bert took a serious pasting, but that was all part of his strategy. Vic wore himself out, delivering a machine-gun-like barrage of forearm smashes to Bert's grizzled face.

Then it was Bert's turn . . .

What happened next is the stuff of grunt 'n' groan folklore. Short story shorter: Vic did not make it back to the dressing room without assistance. He didn't wrestle again for three months.

The roar of that crowd was the future, beckoning Jonny to another world. That was the event that sealed his fate: the night he saw an escape from the coal mines that had claimed generations of his family's men.

Paulie had recently recovered from a serious bout of Polio and bought himself a motorbike to celebrate. Letters from Brynmawr outlined plans to ride down for a visit. Paulie was the only one who knew about the wedding, and Jonny swore him to secrecy in his last letter.

Jonny watches the door glumly. The day remains Paulieless.

But there is Jane.

She sits behind the big table, attended to by her solitary bridesmaid—the jewel in the crown of the house of Porter. Her dark brown hair is all done up into a towering beehive—that pink lipstick, inevitably applied—those eye sapphires flit at Jonny from time to time as he sits beside her. In that dress, she looks like she's stepped out of a Chuck Berry song: Jonny's sweet little rock 'n' roller . . . his little queenie.

The afternoon drags itself into the evening and all Jonny can think about is being alone with his bride in that dress. Every second that bed in the other room lies empty is an affront to the laws of desire.

There are raised voices from the bar below, but no one, as far as Jonny could make out, has been chinned. Finally, ten o'clock crawls upon them. The pub is closing, Danny spins a final Guy Mitchell record, and Jonny accepts brisk and brief congratulations from people he has no expectations of seeing again.

Finally, they are alone, and Jonny leads his bride down a dim corridor to their room and their first night of forever.

'No, leave it on.'

'What?'

'Leave the dress on.'

'Why?' she says, suspiciously.

'Because you look fucking incredible in it.'

Jonny pulls her hard towards him. 'Looking at you all day in that dress and all I could think about was now. Us, alone, with you in it.'

He places one hand on her hip and winds his other around her back and zips it up.

'No,' her shoulders wiggle an escape, 'it'll get messed up.'

Jonny will not be denied and nuzzles into her neck—pulling delicately on her lobe with his teeth. 'It won't get messed up, I promise'

The heady combination of the day-long booze on her breath and the taste of waxy lipstick on his mouth is a brew made in Asgard.

She surrenders to the moment . . . for a moment. Then sense ascends. 'No. Let me take it off.'

Within a minute, they are naked in the narrow bed. In accord with the gods of social expectation, this is their first legitimate intimacy, but as they rock and roll, Jonny stares glumly at the dress folded neatly over the chair.

Twenty minutes later, they lie in silence. Jonny assumes she's asleep until she asks, 'What's the matter with you?'

They were joined in holy matrimony now, so should be able to talk about anything. This didn't stop the next words out of his mouth from being delivered with great effort. 'Even if it did get messed up—*which it wouldn't have done*—so what? You weren't planning on wearing it again, were you?'

She turns away from the wall to face him, dumping her supporting elbow hard into the pillow. 'You *still* on about that dress?'

Jonny lets out a long, slow, gargantuan, defeated sigh. 'Didn't seem a lot to ask, that's all. I should imagine there'll be more important things we'll want from each other as time goes on. Great fucking start, this is.'

'You're unbelievable!'

'You better believe it. Go to sleep.'

Jane turns back away from him. 'Suit yourself!'

Jonny convinced himself that there being no punch-up at the reception—that this union was not blessed with bloodshed—was a bad omen. He had no idea that glum, vacant, distracted sex was possible. He never knew you could drift off to sleep seething with rage.

On his wedding night, he learns both of these things.

He had anticipated the difficulty of getting any sleep in that narrow prison-like bed, but as his burgeoning consciousness negotiates with this pale April morning, he knows for sure. Jane, however, knows no such thing as she sleeps as solidly as his raging neglected hard on—roaring silently beneath the sheets like an Oscar awarded to *worst wedding night of 1963* ...

And the winner is ...

This reminds him ...

She begins to stir. Jonny already has his day mapped out.

Go over to Brixton. Find Hammerstone headquarters and impose himself directly. Then, in the interests of celebrations or commiserations, hit Soho and see if he can find Brenda, his little on/off situation who worked as a waitress at Coffeeville when she wasn't auditioning somewhere. She was a dancer on the *Cool for Cats* television show until they took it off and now her life was an endless parade of casting calls and walk-on's. They'd never sealed the deal, but it was always waiting in the wings. They also had something in common—she was as interested in girls as he was. '*Look at the tits on that!*' was a familiar declaration from out the girl's mouth whenever a worthy contender infringed on Brenda's eye line. And after last night's wedding night let down, Jonny is in desperate need of a more animated female presence.

So much for the focus.

The one-woman-man shtick.

But it's against nature, though, *right*?

It's nearly ten now. The day is escaping him. Time to get with it.

Jane stretches deliciously, as if recent events are a thing to be happy about. She takes a moment to get her bearings in the unfamiliar room and joins the day. 'So, what are we doing today, then?'

Jonny is already half-dressed, in his Y-fronts, shirt and socks, and making tea. This strikes him as faintly absurd. Why the fuck is *he* making the tea? *She* should be doing this. Such is the price of moving things along.

Make tea.

Get out of here.

Get on.

'I told you. I've got to go over to Brixton.'

'On a Sunday?'

'Yeah, on a Sunday. It's a wresting promoter's, not a shop.'

He brings the tea over and is about to place it on the chair, but thinks better of it. 'Better not put it there, eh? Don't wanna get tea on the dress.'

She looks at him funny and takes the mug, as if she has forgotten all about the dress drama. She had underestimated its importance last night and still does; it seems.

'So,' Jonny turns her question around, 'what are *you* doing today?'

'Thought we'd at least spend it together. Maybe I could come with you.'

'To Hammerstone's? No, this is business. It'd be like taking your girlfriend to a job interview.'

'Wife.'

'Wife—to a job interview. Besides, they don't let birds in.'

'How do you know? I thought you'd never been there.'

'It's a wrestling headquarters. There's probably a gym. Have you ever seen a mixed gym?'

Jane had never seen a gym full-stop. 'So, then what? What are you doing after that?'

'Depends how long they take. It's a Sunday, so it's probably gonna take three buses and half the day to get there.'

'Get a tube.'

'Do they have a tube to Brixton?'

'How should I know? Doubt it.'

'Well then.'

'What about tomorrow?'

'What about it?'

'Whatcha doin'?'

'Going to the Foresters training and make some calls. If things don't pan out at Hammerstone's today for any reason, I'll see if DeMarto's have got anything for me. Anyway, you'll be at work.'

'No, I won't. I left.'

'What? You left? Why?'

'Well, I'm married now, ain't I?'

'What's that got to do with it?'

'When any of the girls get married, they leave. Anyway, I'm due in September, so I'd have to leave soon, anyway.'

'So? That's five months away. My Mam worked right up until a week before she had my sister.'

'That was years ago. It's different now.'

Jonny lifts the dress off the back of the chair, carefully, contemptuously, places it on the end of the bed and sits down to pull his trousers on.

'We're supposed to be saving for a deposit on a flat. We need all the money we can get. So, you need to go back down there, Monday, and get that job back.'

'I can't. What's that gonna look like? I'm gonna look like a right berk.'

'Don't care what it looks like. We need to get somewhere before that baby arrives. And that means you pulling your weight, too.'

'Embarrassing.'

'Well, that's your fault. You shouldn't have left in the first place.'

'Thought the bloke was supposed to go out to work, and the wife looks after the house.'

'When we have a house, great. But that won't happen until we scrape the dough together.' He pulls his plimsolls on, stands up and grabs his jacket. 'You're living in a fucking dream, girl. Get real!'

By the time she yells after him 'Some husband you are!' he's already halfway down the stairs.

4. OVER THE RIVER

He has no idea where Hammerstone Promotions is exactly, but Nicky said it's in Brixton.

Jonny hops off the platform of the 2B bus just after a couple of rivet-peppered steel bridges that seem to hold the two sides of the high street together.

As soon as his plimsolls hit the pavement, he knows this is the route Nicky had taken on the way back from Croydon to Victoria on Friday. Nicky hadn't pointed out the place nor made any mention of its location, which suggests it's somewhere off the main drag. He gets as far as the Rialto Cinema when he realises he will have to start asking people.

The first two passers-by he intercepts have never heard of it. A young Indian-looking woman with two freakishly small kids points out the Town Hall over the crossroads and tells him he should ask there. He looks in the direction of where she's pointing and sees a *very* black man (no cream in this one's coffee) crossing the street towards him. Jonny tries to place him, but the penny is yet to drop. The man senses Jonny's scrutiny and nods a vague hello with his grenade-like head. It's *Bobi "Hammerhead" Ofey*.

'You're Bobi Ofey!'

'Hullo, son.'

'I'm looking for Hammerstone's.'

Bobi wears a chunky yellow jumper with baggy slacks, carrying a small leather case. Jonny notices he's wearing his wrestling boots.

'You're at the wrong end of the road, son. I'm going there now. I'll show you.'

The star and the wannabe walk side-by-side, back in the direction Jonny had come. Excitement rising, this is a real-life wrestling star. He's been on TV! Ofey has everything Jonny wants. He is everything Jonny wants to be. He is *this* close to the light.

'I detect an accent,' Bobi says. 'You Welsh?'

Telling people *Brynmawr* was always a mistake. They'd look at him like he had a speech impediment. So, he always told 'em Cardiff. It was near enough.

'Cardiff, more or less.' Been trying to ditch it—the accent. They hear an accent and it's like, y'know...'

'Yeah, I know.' Bobi side-longs the over-excited hopeful. 'The further away from home you are, the more you should try to hang on to some of it.'

Jonny hadn't crossed the river for any "dad talk". He is here to change his world, and as he walks with Bobi "Hammerhead" Ofey in broad daylight, he feels the earth shift beneath him. 'I've come to see Gil. Or the other one.'

'Jock.'

'Yeah, Jock. Nicky says to go see 'em. You know Nicky Nash?'

'Yeah, we all know Nicky. You know Jock and Gil?'

'Not yet. But they're gonna know me.'

They are acquainted now. Jonny offers his hand. 'I'm Kid "Tarzan" Jonathan.'

Reflex compels Bobi to accept the offer and shakes Jonny's over-firm grip. 'Oh, like Don Leo Jonathan. You like the American guys?'

'Oh yeah. Buddy Rogers, Crazy Luke Graham, Johnny Valentine, Dick the Bruiser... brilliant. All of 'em. When I'm done here—made it here—that's where I'm going, America.

Bobi chuckles deep. 'And when you're done with this planet, then what?'

The man is easy to talk to. If they're all like him at Hammerstone's, stardom could be weeks away. It's not *what* you know...

'Who knows?' Jonny challenged cheerfully. 'I could be fighting you soon.'

'Could be.'

'That'd be a tear up, wouldn't it? Bobi "Hammerhead" Ofey verses Kid "Tarzan" Jonathan in a European championship of the world!'

'European championship? Of the world?'

'You know what I mean. Anyway, why not have a European *and* world championship in one go? Speed things up, wouldn't it?'

'Well . . . you gotta learn to walk before you can run. You have wrestled before, right?'

'Oh yeah. Course. Independents, mainly. You heard of "Gentleman" Joe Malone?'

'No.'

'No? Well, I wrestled him at the New Addington Hotel. Heard of it?'

'No.'

'That was my first ever match.'

'When was that?'

'Three years ago.'

'Three?'

'Amateur circuit. Done loads since, obviously. Thirty-eight matches, for DeMarto's, mainly. Been honing my craft. But I'm ready now. I watch 'em all and I can see I'm there.'

'It's a hard game, but I can see you're serious.' Bobi's yellowy eyes hold Jonny's hopeful blues as they walk.

'You serious?'

'Oh, I'm serious. Serious as gout.'

Jonny marches on a moment as Bobi stops. 'This is it.'

Bobi turns and walks up the stone steps to a wide-open door of what looks, to Jonny's eyes, like an enormous house. 'Good luck.'

This is it?

Hammerstone Promotions.

313 Brixton Road.

The gateway to stardom.

Bobi goes straight on in. Jonny hesitates. He wants to savour the moment. This door is the portal through which his destiny awaits. He steps over the threshold, into the future. A dusty, threadbare carpeted hallway leads into a spit 'n' sawdust gymnasium. The first one he sees is Nicky on the payphone, who nods a cool hello. Nearby are a couple of girls Jonny will later learn are wrestling groupies, Doreen and Claire. Claire: imaginatively known as 'The One-Armed Bandit' on account of the fact that her left arm is missing just below the elbow.

Doreen puts it to Nicky. 'Are you going to be much longer on that phone?'

Nicky hangs up and as he dials another number, smiles pleasantly and suggests she 'Fuck off.'

The atmosphere is thick with cigarette smoke despite the NO SMOKING signs everywhere. Dirty-white painted brick walls are obscured with wrestling posters, yellowing with antiquity. In the centre of the gym is a full-size ring with mats and barbells scattered around it.

The place is busy. Most of the boys are here, but only Vampyre Ken and Terrence "Hooray" Buckingham are in the ring, having a pull around. Any excuse to get out of the house, so most of the men are here for a Sunday morning parade and to chitty chat. Until, that is, Gil Stone in a Lonsdale sweater and baggy sweatpants, black strands of thin hair traverse a large perspiring head, comes down from the office and calls the room to attention. 'Ladies!'

Everyone stops what they're not doing and congregates around him. Jonny hangs back, eager to be privy to a real wrestler's conference.

Gil makes a mental manifest as to who's in attendance. He sees Doreen and the One-Armed Bandit. 'You two! Piss off!'

'But we're with Damien!' Doreen whines.

Gil locates Damien Logan, one of the 'big dick' dazzlers, finishing up on the bench press. 'Don't bring your tarts in here, Dame.' He turns back to the girls. 'Leave!'

The girls mutter and do so. Gil clocks Jonny with faint recognition but ignores him.

Jonny takes, spins, and sits astride a chair in the far corner next to Kareem, The Egyptian Magician.

The office door opens once again and Gil's senior partner and brother-in-law, Jock Hammer, greying shock of quiffed hair, still in formidable shape and, for once, not dressed in an immaculate black whistle but in a freshly ironed red track-suit, comes out, takes a chair, turns it round and sits astride it, a la Jonny.

These men do not sit like other men.

Gil speaks. 'Right, first things first. Dom's still in a coma. Obviously, he won't be earning anytime soon, so we're having a collection for his missus. I'll leave an envelope hanging on the office door. Please give generously!'

Jonny whispers for affirmation from Kareem. 'Still in a coma?!'

'Seems so.'

Gil changes tack. 'Right! Everyone form a line.'

Everyone standing does so.

Gil scans anxious faces. 'Right. All of you who are currently working for Hammerstone Promotions, please take one step forward.'

Kareem stage whispers to all within his vicinity. 'Here we go—elimination time.'

All the wrestlers take a step forward.

With a thick finger, Gil points at "Dazzler" Damien Logan. 'What the fuck are *you* doing?'

'What?'

Someone laughs. Probably Evan Leigh.

Gil reiterates. 'I said, all those *currently* working.'

'Don't be funny, Gil.'

Gil's eyes narrow, like a sniper getting a bead on his target. 'Reliability and at least *some* wrestling ability is all we ask. You gotta be reliable, and you are the most unreliable cunt in the universe. Hence, the boot.'

'Gil, you're having a laugh. I told you, my car—'

'I don't wanna hear it, *Dame*. It's one fucking excuse after another. You almost missed your match on Friday, again! We don't need the tension.'

'The match got cancelled anyway, so what's the fucking difference?'

'That's beside the point! You *cannot* be relied upon. You're out.'

Damien knows Gil and his tight-arse brother-in-law well enough to know further protest is futile, so takes it on the toes, makes for the door and shouts back, 'Fuck you, Gil! You can't sack me, I'm jacking it in any way, so fuck off!'

It's a lame response, and everyone knows it. But in lieu of anything more devastating, it serves as Damien Logan's swansong as far as the world of wresting is concerned.

Gil affects a tight-lipped smile until Damien has vacated the premises. 'Right. Putting that unpleasantness behind us, I have a question for you all.'

The men shuffle collectively ... uncomfortably.

'Are you actors or athletes?'

A collective groan.

The Egyptian pipes up. 'Is this the equity thing again?'

'Yes, it is,' Gil answers. 'Nicely anticipated, Mr Rizk.'

Evan speaks. 'They're still dragging this out?'

'Yes, they are. Again, it's the television people kicking off about the fact that we're getting an hour of their prime time every Saturday while none of us are answerable to their fucking union.'

That groan again.

Jock enters the fray, standing up and stepping in front of his junior partner. 'We've been on that phone all week—like we've got nothing else better to do—and explained our position again. And *again*, they're not having any of it. Now the only reason we've managed to avoid this bollocks up 'till now is 'cos we've stuck together on this, okay? At the end of the day, they want us, we want them, and as long as we stand fast and insist this is a bona fide sport and not a pissin' panto, then we should be able to retain our integrity as it were. And that *is* what we're dealing with here girls, our—*your*—integrity.'

Gil brings it home. 'The public see wrestlers joining an actor's union and the message we send out to millions is—?'

Terry "Hooray" Buckingham murmurs. 'That the game's a fucking con.'

'Right,' Gil concurs.

Someone at the back says, 'That it ain't a sport, it's a—'

'It *says* it's a farce,' Gil interrupts. 'Theatre. It's akin to admitting that the game is fixed.'

Lincoln, one of the Atomic Twins, shouts, 'It *is* fixed!'

Jock is quick to fuck Lincoln off. 'Is that a fact? Then you better tell Dom's missus that he's only faking his coma to avoid her.'

'Plausible,' Evan mutters.

'*Shut up*!' Gil yells.

'Thing is,' Vampyre Ken counters, 'if we *do* join equity, won't that make getting acting work easier?'

'*Acting work*?' Jock answers, incredulously, eyeing the Vampyre.

'Yeah.'

Jock looks back at Gil, who shrugs, then scans the room. 'Who's been offered acting work?'

Silence reigns.

'Well then,' Jock concludes, 'I don't think anyone'll be leaving us to be the next Troy Donahue just yet then, do you?'

Nicky hangs up the phone and catches the gist of the conference.

Vampyre Ken says, 'Nothing wrong with keeping your options open, though, is there?'

'Options?' Jock scoffs. 'Listen, if we're not giving you enough work, take it on the fucking arches and try DeMarto's. They're cryin' out for fighters!'

'Yeah, says Ken, dejectedly. 'But they ain't got the telly, have they?'

'There you go!' says Jock. '*This*'—he stabs towards the floor with a gnarly finger—'is where the action is.'

Nicky leans back with his arms crossed by the wall phone. He shouts over the demurring crowd. 'Course, this 'ain't got nothing to do with the fact that if these boys were in a union, you'd have to put 'em on a minimum earner, would it?'

The boys turn around, seeing Nicky standing there, besuited, smirking.

Jock side-spits at Gil, 'Who the fuck's that?'

Gil addresses the dissent. 'Nick, why don't you mind your own business? You got fuck all to do with this, so—'

Nicky laughs that chokey laugh. 'Sorry Gil, your conscience must have got the better of me for a minute there.'

Jock asks again, 'Gil, who *is* that?'

'It's Nick. Nick the prick. Connected.'

Jock appraises the interloper with a flinty eye and mutters to Gil out the side of his mouth. 'Oh, *that's* him, is it? I'll connect the four-eyed cunt to the floor.'

Gil appeals to the crowd once more. 'So, girls, I'm gonna leave this clipboard hanging here outside the office with this petition. I suggest you express your desires and sign the fuckin' thing, for what it's worth. Who knows, it might shut 'em up for five minutes.'

He gives the hesitant men five seconds to respond. 'Anything else? No? Good. Now, piss off. And *don't* forget Dom!'

The wrestlers go back to their talking and training and smoking and smoking and training and talking...

Jock and Gil go up to the office. Jonny looks over at Nicky, who, whilst dialling another number, gives Jonny the nod and mouths a silent, '*Go on up.*'

Jonny watches the men disappear into their office; gives them a minute; steels himself and follows them up.

He knocks and enters. Jock is on the phone, doing more listening than talking. Gil is arranging the 'cards' for forthcoming events, papers spread across his desk.

'Alright, Gil. Jock.'

Jock, intent on whatever he's being told on the phone, ignores him. It takes Gil a moment to remember who this interloper is. He doesn't, entirely. Then he does . . . ahhh, Nicky's little mate from the Fairfield.

'Alright? *Kid*, is it?"

'So, when are you gonna give me a match then?'

'We'll letcha know.'

'Why don't we go out there now—have a shoot—so I can show you what I can do. I'm better than all them cunts.'

'You can shoot?'

'*Can I shoot*? I'm a son of a gun, me!'

'I'm sure you're just poetry in motion out there, kid, but you put some guys in front of a crowd and they just freeze up. We gotta see you out in the field.'

'Put me in the field then!'

'Who you wrestling for now?'

'DeMarto's. Among others.'

'Well, there you go!' Gil declares, brightly, but giving Jock the wink. 'Next time you're working, give us a shout and one of us'll try'n come down.'

'You sure you can't fit me in?'

'Sorry mate, not at the moment.'

Jonny didn't want to pull this gun, but desperation dictates he must.

'Nicky sent me.'

'Nicky?'

'Said to have a word. Said you own him a favour.' He lets this appreciate. 'I s'pose I'm the favour.'

Jock comes off the phone and casts a practised eye over the youngster. 'You're too young and you're too small!'

'I'll get older,' Jonny retorts. 'And bigger, too. And you haven't seen me fight.'

Jock nods at Jonny and turns to Gil. 'This your mate, Nick's boy?'

'He's not my mate.'

Jonny chimes in, 'I'm not Nick's boy.'

Jock regards the two men with amusement. Somehow, these two idiots have got themselves juiced into the local firm. He will un-juice Gil once the nature of his involvement becomes clear. But the kid can be dealt with immediately.

'Gil, what are we doing about Damien's slot on Saturday?'

'Haven't had a chance to sort that out yet.'

Jock says to Jonny. 'Can you make it to Catford, Saturday night? Lewisham Concert Hall.'

'For a match?'

'Yeah, a match.'

'Fucking yeah. No problem.'

'You'll be on with Kelly Hewitt, though.'

The image of a mangled Dominic "The Dominator" Farrago tubed up in a hospital bed attempts to derail Jonny's resolve.

Fuck it.

'Hewitt don't scare me. He's an old man. Should have packed it up years ago.'

On the one hand, Jock pulling rank yet again, is an annoyance, but on the other . . . Gil's seen 'em come and go—mouthy little dreamers, giving it the big one—ending up, three matches later, back on the building site they should never have left in the first place. But then . . . the distinct certitude of this little twat winding up in a hospital bed next to the Dominator is cause for a giggle.

'You even know where Catford is?'

'Catford? Yeah. Near Crystal Palace, ain't it?'

'Yeah, Jonny. More or less. Give or take Sydenham.'

'Right then. We'll put you on with Kelly Hewitt in Catford. Yeah, Jock? Saturday night. Don't fuck it up. Our ears are radar-like, and our eyes are telescopic. '

Jonny backs away to the door, before they change their minds, fearing that to break eye-contact will break the spell that has landed him this bona fide shot.

'Catford then. Saturday.'

Gil comes over and guides Jonny towards the door. On reflex, he flexes a bicep.

'Nice arm,' Gil admits.

'The rest of me's a bit of alright 'an all.'

Gil opens the door, guides him through it and goes back to his desk.

The men have already forgotten him as they busy themselves with maps and calendars and the arcane machinations of venue hire.

The door closes on Jonny's 'Saturday then!'

All the Hammerstone wrestlers hang out at Vern's—a greasy-spoon café on the other side of the high street—the kind of cholesterol fest that only the supremely athletic can survive.

Vern, an ancient Jamaican in a big woollen hat, busies himself behind his counter with a sus roll up in his mouth, bashing a mountain of spuds.

Derek and Patsy's calypso-style *Housewife's Choice* is rendered a tinny crackle from a single speaker rigged up to a bulky reel-to-reel tape recorder on the counter. Reggae is yet to happen. We are on the eve of Ska.

There are no women in the place. Not even Doreen and the Bandit, who are probably licking Damien Logan's wounds somewhere. Men lay siege to the counter. Others demolish pile-'em-high fry-ups and huge pies with chips and beans. The usual fog of cigarette smoke is, this time, made more intense by the steam from the espresso machine.

Jonny recognises the music from that blues party he went to—the kind that rattles windows over in Kensal Rise. He takes his frothy coffee over to the table, where Evan stares vacantly out of the window. For a man who lives and dies on his last one-liner, Evan is all melancholia when devoid of an audience. Jonny remembered someone telling him about class clowns. *You don't wanna be around when the laughter stops.*

Jonny pops Evan's doom balloon. 'Why'd he do that? Sack the bloke in front of everyone? Made him look a right cunt.'

Evan ignores his dried cheese sandwich and stirs his tea while watching a gaggle of teenage girls coming down the steps of the police station across the road. One girl is in tears and the others, holding her hands, are consoling her.

Evan taps his spoon on the edge of the mug. *Tink Tink Tink*, heralds his response. 'It's how they operate. If anyone takes the piss—or is even *thought* to be taking the piss—then said piss taker must be taken in hand. And a little humiliation thrown into the mix can help seal the deal. It's the only way to maintain the SQ.'

Jonny knows all about the SQ and its maintenance, and wonders if he and Nicky's message the other day was enough to convince Samuel Fortnoy to adhere to said status quo.

'Seems to be a lot of that,' Jonny muses. 'A lot of maintaining the SQ.'

Evan slurps his hot drink—smacks his lips with satisfaction. 'It's either that or chaos. You can appreciate that, can't ya? Got to have order or no-one knows where they are.'

Jonny considers this—nods agreement and turns to happier tidings. 'They gave me a match.'

'Oh yeah? Where?'

'Catford. Saturday. With Kelly Hewitt.'

For the first time, Jonny has truly gotten Evan's attention. 'Why the fuck would they put you on with *him*? Who have you upset?'

'Emergency fill in. Now they've got rid of Logan.'

'Yeah, but . . . why you? You know Hewitt fucked Dom in Croydon last week? Yeah, 'course you do. You were there.'

'I saw 'em carrying him out, yeah.'

'Becoming a regular occurrence of late, Hewitt's excesses.' Evan sips loudly on his tea. 'He's a cunt's hair away from criminal proceedings, that one. Now why would they put you on with him, though? That's just . . . spiteful.'

'From what I can make out, Gil owes Nicky a favour, so he gave me a shot.'

'Nicky who? Nash?'

'Yeah.'

'Gotcha.'

'What?'

They might *owe* Nicky, but they don't *like* him. And what they don't like even more than Nicky Nash, is *owing* Nicky Nash. Clearly, they don't think much of you either, probably because of your affiliation with said four-eyed cunt. So, saying yeah to Nicky gets them off of whatever hooks they're on.'

'That Gil's on.'

'That Gil's on . . . and your extermination at the hands of that total fucking nutcase gets you out of their faces, too.'

Vern's has no shitter and Jonny needs to go. He knocks back the dregs of his coffee.

'See you in Catford.'

'Yeah, see ya. Watch yourself. Hewitt's a section 8 psycho.'

'He don't scare me.'

'Good for you, Jonny. The graveyard's full of the brave.'

5. COME DANCING

It was one of *those* nights.

The ones with pieces missing.

The ones with big dark irretrievable chunks of fearful occurrence ... gone.

The ones that end in ways Jonny would have laughed at if it wasn't so hysterically grim.

Never in his wildest dreams ...

The morning of his first fight for Hammerstone Promotions began agreeably enough.

He was up at six in the AM.

Went for a run through the neighbourhood and around Little Wormwood Recreational Grounds. He kept the workout afterwards to a minimum. Although his bluster to Jock and Gill was tempered with an unshakable self-belief, he knew Hewitt would be a handful and didn't want to leave his fight at home.

His run took him down along the canal and over the cobbled stones of Kensal Rise, but he avoided Octavia House. He hadn't seen Jane since the morning after the wedding and part of him couldn't give a fuck. But only a small part. The rest of him—the big part, still wanted her. She made the idea of not wanting anyone else—if not easy—easier. Then there was the kid. The one on the way. The fact he wasn't more available bugged him. But then he thought of the future and the big deal that that kid's dad would be one day. This justified everything. He'd be someone to be proud of. Not like *his* old man ...

He went over there, Wednesday afternoon, to Octavia, with every intention of knocking on the door and taking her for a *let's bury the hatchet* night out to the pictures. But as he approached the dark, imposing monolith at the end of

West Row, he felt as if he was dashing into a dark labyrinth of cunt-struck oblivion.

No.

Not Jonny.

She was the one that was being stupid.

Let her make it right.

Wife or no wife.

Kid or no kid.

If it wasn't for tonight's fight, he might have wobbled. Luckily, he had that to galvanise his resolve, to keep him on the straight.

Now the day had arrived. He left early. Lucky really. It took a tube to New Cross Gate, a bus and a couple of hours to get him across the city until he finds himself hopping onto Catford Road outside the venue.

This is it.

His first match for the big boys.

He stands before the poster outside the building—a church-sized donut's worth of Art déco—glancing around to see if anyone else beholds this soon-to-be historical tract. Apart from a small queue at the box office, the high street proceeds untroubled, but there he is—right at the bottom—vs. Kelly Hewitt. Bottom of the bill: it seems Hewitt has been demoted, probably for that Croydon mess, but . . . for Jonny, it's happening.

Saturday 4th May. Lewisham Concert Hall

KELLY HEWITT
vs.
KID "TARZAN" JONATHAN

Gil Stone catches up with him at the dressing room door, begrudgingly impressed that the kid has turned up at all. Was Hewitt's rep really lost on this idiot? If it wasn't for the endgame in mind, he might have felt sorry for the young, dumb sap. 'Where's your boots, son?'

'I fight without 'em. It's part of my image.'

'*Part* of it? What else?'

'My name,' Jonny proclaims proudly. 'Kid "Tarzan" Jonathan.'

'*That's* your image? Someone else's name and no boots?'

'Tarzan don't wear boots.'

'E don't wrestle in Catford niver!'

Jonny has to ask. '*W*hatcha mean, someone else's name?'

'*Don Leo Jonathan?*'

The twat is hip, Jonny thinks. '*You've* heard of him?'

'Yeah, I've heard of him. Lucky 'e's on the other side of the drink or 'e'll be after ya for nicking his name. You got a towel at least?'

'Yeah, I got a towel.'

'Get out there, then. C'mon! Quick smart!'

Catford's Lewisham Concert Hall is not exactly the Fairfield, but this is a Hammerstone promotion! The Fairfield will come later. Fuck it. Jonny will be at the Albert Hall before the year's out. By then, he'd be able to afford all the boots in the world and wouldn't have to lie about their lack, thereof, being part of his image.

Jonny's been given the decision. Hewitt to take the fall. To humiliate him, probably. But Jonny requires no validation from the Hammerstone gods. He's gonna hit Hewitt early. Hit him hard. Show him what's what.

But best laid plans and all that . . .

'A-ladies and a-gentlemen! Hammerstone Promotions welcome you to an evening of professional wrestling in the official Lord Mount-Evans style! In the blue corner, weighing in at sixteen stones and two—from Bradford . . . Kelly Hewitt!!!'

The crowd boos and jeers. Hewitt is above it. He runs his gnarly hands through his already sweaty hair and wipes them together.

As Jonny faces Hewitt, the man seems vacant, as if he just remembered he'd left the gas on at home. He's about 5.9, solidly built but running to fat and is wearing plain red trunks. Nothing about the man tallies with his fearsome rep.

'And in the red corner, making his Hammerstone debut, weighing in at twelve stone . . . from Cardiff, Wales . . . Kid "Tarzan" Jonathan!'

The crowd applauds, politely. Someone whistles. Jonny hopes it's a girl and flashes a smile in the direction from where it came.

It's happening.
It's happening.
It's happening.

'This contest will be decided in five six-minute rounds! Two falls, two submissions or a knockout to decide the winner!'

Geoff the M.C vacates the ring and referee Reg steps in and does his thing. He pulls the fighters into a huddle, checks their nails and recites the party line. 'No gauging. No bulling. No hair pulling and you break when I say break. Go to your corners.'

Jonny tries in vain to catch Hewitt's eye. Jonny will not be rendered invisible, but the man seems to be looking right through him.

Like he isn't here.

Well, he *is* here alright, and this big fat prick is about to find out just how much.

The bell clangs . . .

Oooooof! Jonny's opening forearm-smash is a direct hit, straight across Hewitt's chops, but the man just takes it and staggers back a step. Jonny is unsure whether the smattering of laughter from the crowd is due to Hewitt's comical stagger or the total ineffectiveness of Jonny's attack. Jonny reaches deep into his repertoire. Hewitt slips out and away from every hold he tries—and that annoying *I'm-not-quite-here demeanour*! Jonny might just as well as be fighting himself.

But then, another forearm-smash changes everything.

Unfortunately, it isn't one of Jonny's...

He tries to make sense of the lights hanging high above him, like electric sign-post quasars to Elysian Fields. Then the realisation creeps upon him—that he is flat out on his back.

The hurting hasn't arrived yet.

But it's in the post.

No question.

And there it is...

Is it snapped off?

The left side of his jaw?

Detached from whatever it was supposed to be fixed to?

Stabs of agony rise with the volume of the jeering, cheering crowd.

Random recollections of the days leading up to this moment flash and tumble over themselves, jostling for his scrambled attention.

Then he hears it: the count. *...four...three...two...*

It isn't strength, or adrenaline, or reflex that puts him back on his feet before the referee confirms his defeat.

It's *heart*. And Jonny has *heart* in abundance.

He shakes out the shock on unsteady bare feet and tries to get a fix on his opponent, who he feels circling around him, appraising his stance, his positioning, perusing the menu of Kid "Tarzan" Jonathan's annihilation.

Hewitt makes that clumsy "signature-move" grab for Jonny's legs—the one that put the Dominator in hospital.

Jonny doesn't see or even feel what happens next.

Later, he will remember the roar of the crowd—the screeching hags, the rattle of thrown metal chairs as they bounce on the mat around him . . .

The next thing he knows—knows for sure—is coming around in the back seat of a moving car. Someone had dressed him.

Evan's Zephyr takes a sharp right at Forest Hill and descends west towards night-time Streatham. That's when Jonny—jammed as he is between Vampyre Ken and The Egyptian Magician—starts to get his bearings.

Geographically . . .

Mentally . . .

'You sure he's alright?'

It's Ian, in the front passenger seat—one of the ring rats. 'Jonny. You alright?'

Evan gets a fix on Jonny in the rear-view mirror. 'Well, he's in better nick than ol' Dom is, that's for sure. At least he ain't in a coma.'

'You alright, Jonny?' Ian reiterates.

Jonny knows he's been asked this question numerous times already. It's only now that he understands it. 'Yeah yeah. Why'd you keep asking me?'

'Cos you keep not answering, *numb nuts*. Thought you might have concussion. Was gonna take you to A & E.'

Jonny comes around a little bit and makes a quick itinerary of who he is making this journey with. 'Where we goin'?'

Evan jumps a red, narrowly missing a bus. 'We're going drinking, that's where. You could use one.'

'I can't afford to be boozing . . .' Gathering sentience makes a new ascension. 'Where's my money? Did they pay me?'

Ian hands Jonny a folded brown envelope. 'There you go.'

With relief, Jonny takes it, peers in and sees the four green notes he is expecting. He stuffs the envelope deep into his jeans pocket. 'Surprised they coughed up after that lot.'

Evan finds Jonny in the rear-view again. 'You did good, mate. Gave a good account of yourself. If the idea was to discourage ya, they got it oh so fucking wrong. As you can imagine, they're having a tough time finding opponents for Hewitt—especially after that Croydon fuck up. You stepped up. That's gotta make an impression.'

'D' ya hear?' Ian says to all. 'Dom's missus is trying to do Hewitt for G.B.H.'

'She should thank her lucky stars it ain't for manslaughter,' Evan answers.

'Cunt', says the Egyptian.

'Fuck that!' Ken protests. 'She got every right to be miffed.'

'Not *her*,' Evan corrects him. '*Hewitt*!'

'Cunt, indeed,' Evan concurs.

'My fucking head,' Jonny groans.

'Nothing a straight Johnny Walker won't fix,' says Vampyre Ken.

'I think my neck's broken.'

'Shut up. You did good.'

'I did shit.'

'Hewitt's a lunatic and you went in with him. That's gonna look good. Shows balls.'

The Egyptian turns to Jonny. 'I hear Jock and Gill are fucking you about.'

'Jock's alright, but that Gil's an arsehole. He's got some fuckin' problem with me.'

'Don't worry about him. Gil's got second-in-command syndrome. Thinks he should be running the show but just hasn't got Jock's *in*—his expertise—his knowing how to play people.'

'Jock—he's a fucking chess player, the bloke,' offers Ian, helpfully. 'A genius in his way. There's a reason

Hammerstone's is *the* top promotion in the South, and that reason is Jock Hammer.'

'It's the telly,' Evan says. 'Since Jock got the game on the box, they've been swamped with people trying to get in on it. But now every cunt with no trousers on thinks they can wrestle. And it's *their* job—Jock and Gil—to keep the riffraff out, know what I mean? It's just that Jock's got a talent for spotting talent. Gil's an also ran in that regard, but it's only everyone else that knows it.'

Jonny peers through the car's window, trying to get his bearings from a dark and untamed land they call West Dulwich. 'Five years I've been down here and I'm still poncing about going nowhere.'

'Maybe you should get a gimmick,' Evan suggests. 'A new image.'

'Don't need one. I can actually wrestle—better than *all* them cunts. Doesn't that count for something? I mean, look at the Dominator. If he could still wrestle properly, he wouldn't be in a coma.'

'He was a great wrestler', The Egyptian asserts. 'He just milked it and came unstuck, that's all. Gotta know when it's time to call it a night.'

They are in Streatham now. Back in the day, this was the place to be—*The West End of the South!*—whatever that meant. Unless, of course, you had better things to do in the West End. Nowadays, *everyone's* got better things to do in the West end.

They get pissed in the Horse and Groom pub, leave Ian and Ken waiting for some birds they've arranged to meet, then Evan and Kareem take Jonny up the road a bit, to the Locarno night club.

COME DANCING, the big bulb-encrusted sign across the edifice of the building announces loudly and proudly.

MECCA DANCING, the sign below adds, specifically . . . helpfully . . . confusingly . . .

The Locarno Ballroom exists in that uncertain void between its pre-war glory days of the big band era and these waning days of Rock 'n' Roll. Haunted by Ruth Ellis, they say. She was a waitress here, apparently, before serving her last Daiquiri and waltzing off with the dubious accolade of being the last woman in England to be *hung by the neck until dead.*

The vast dance floor is busy with dribblers. Toni Fisher's *Big Hurt* rhumbas its way out of the speakers for the erection section, the slow creep for the saps, during which they will make their move and claim that bird they've been clocking all night, with now-or-never appeals of the '*Wanna go back to my place*' variety. *My place* being the car in a nearby side-street or alleyway.

There are a few faces in: some T.V stars, footballers and local gangsters. And Damien! The recently redundant Damien Logan bounds over to where the boys are propped up against the bar, talking to a couple of girls.

'Hey, boys! Ladies'

Liv is tall but built. Like a PE teacher on the razzle.
Maybe she is. The boys wonder if those full lips write cheques their owner is prepared to cash.

Marina is short, dark and curvy. The tight Prince-of-Wales-checked pencil skirt is the stuff of universal wank-banks. The glasses render her a nerd-bird. Nerd-birds unnerve the boys. Does the face furniture make her an easier or more troublesome conquest? She's either desperate or too smart for these smack-offs.

'We're having one more here,' Liv announces, 'then we're off up west.'

Evan, captivated by Liv's promising mouth, addresses it—the mouth—almost ignoring the woman it belongs to. 'Getting' late innit? Where to, specifically?'

'Dunno yet. Probably the Cromwellian.'

'Dame, whotcha reckon? Wanna come?'

Damien, resigned to the strong possibility that Liv is already bagged, scopes the room for other prey before his gaze lands discreetly back on Marina's arse.

'Sounds alright. Where's Jonny?'

'Wasn't he with your mate?' Evan asks the girls.

Marina is petite and pretty, despite the glasses. Prettier than Liv, but somehow the taller woman's stature humbles her with the fact that she's the backup and Liv's the main feature.

Marina speaks quietly, as if around her humility. 'I think he was talking to Barb. Don't know where they went.'

'I doubt if he'd be up for it anyway, Dame', says Evan.

'Why? What's up with him?'

'It was his try-out tonight, and they put him on with Hewitt and he got fucking hammered. Obviously, they did it on purpose, thinking he'd get fucked. They've done it before. That's how they lose the riffraff.'

'Cunt!' Damien protests. 'That was supposed to be my match.'

'Yeah, well, you dodged a bullet there, luv.'

It was the legs Jonny had noticed first as she stood drinking from a large wine glass at the bar. No-one noticed them noticing each other, locking lustful eyes with instant mutual understanding. Within two minutes, this understanding had ushered them both into a ladies' toilet cubicle.

The girl possesses a glamour-model's physique and could probably be one if not for the pock-marked hollow of her cheeks. Her red beehive hairdo is piled high but coming apart. She tugs her tight black dress up around her waist. Jonny jams his hand between her pale legs. 'What's a nice place like this doing in a girl like you?'

'Thanks-a-fucking lot,' she gasps. 'A girl could take that the wrong way.'

'What way's that then?'

Those legs are now wrapped around him, and his piercing headache migrates south to an agreeable siege that demands entry. Flies ripped open; he finds himself home. That first entry into undiscovered territory . . . That first grip and lift of soft, illicit thigh . . .

'Oh, you fucker!' she gasps again.

Out in the bar, the boy's safari continues.

Evan says, 'What did you say your names were again?'

'I'm Liv.'

'And I'm Marina . . . for the *eighth* time.'

She's left herself open. Evan's in like Flynn. 'So, Marina, mind if I park my boat?'

In the ladies, Jonny's knee trembler is in full swing. The increasing frequency of thuds from their endeavours inspires the girl in the next cubicle to yell, 'You dirty cunts!'

Jonny and the girl's banging and animalistic grunts alert and alarm.

Bouncers come.

Brute force in tuxes.

Boom! Boom! Boom!

Loud thumps on the cubicle door.

'Fuck off!' Jonny yells. I'm in the middle of someone here!'

Jonny and his conquest lock eyes—his steely lust-filled blues; her emerald lust-filled greens—and stifle mutual giggles.

The lock cracks off its hinges. The door comes flying in and two dickie-bowed meatheads get their fingers into the neck of Jonny's shirt and drag him out. All his limbs flail out wildly and take their chances. Some connect. Most don't. Three girls who had been fixing their makeup are trapped between the fight and the furthest wall from the exit. Jonny's conquest joins them, straightening her dress.

With a hard thud, a bouncer hits a tiled wall and slides down it.

One-by-one, the three girls filter past the action and escape until only Jonny's conquest remains, watching the fight with rapt fascination. Jonny, realising that his diminishing dick is still hanging out, tucks it away. The second bouncer comes for him. Jonny catches him by the collar and half lifts/half throws him through another cubicle door where they land on top of another startled girl struggling to pull her knickers up. Jonny uses the momentum of their fall to force his opponent's head down the toilet and follows this with a series of blows until his man is out cold.

As Jonny races out of the cubicle to the exit, the first bouncer comes around and makes a clumsy grab for his left leg as he leaps over him. Jonny avoids this, turns, and kicks his assailant full in the face with his right.

The boys at the bar are well oiled now and are on one.

Evan's hitting his stride. 'It must take ages to dye your roots that colour', he quips to Liv.

Damien giggles on cue. The hilarity is generating its own steam.

Liv is not impressed. '*Funny.*'

'I'm sorry. C'mon, let's make up. Give us a kiss.'

'Piss off.'

'Alright then, stay a frog.'

Damien's giggle takes off into a full-throated wheeze.

Marina struggles to suppress her amusement. She nudges Damien. 'Your mate's a bit of a comedian, 'ain't he?'

Liv's disgust is palatable. '*Sensational.*'

Damien tries to ride Evan's fun train—it's always a comedy smack-down between these two. 'Everyone says he should be on the stage . . . first one out of town!'—and gets the thunder he desires.

Liv, tired of this skit, asks with ramped up impatience, 'Where the fuck's Barbara?'

Evan sees Jonny first, running for the entrance. 'I dunno, but there's Jonny.'

Jonny shouts as he runs past. 'Must dash!'

The doorman, like a bulldog in a dickie-bow—his fat head purple with bloodlust—chases Jonny along Streatham High Road. Damien and Evan are in hot pursuit. The two wrestlers are chasing the doorman, who stops and turns to face his pursuers.

Evan steps towards him, both fists ready for mayhem. 'C'mon then, fruit cake, let's have ya!'

Jonny returns. The chase reverses and now it's the doorman who is being chased back to the club by three pissed-up wrestlers.

Laughing hysterically, they slow down to a brisk pace, letting their quarry escape.

'You cunt!' Evan says, 'We were bang on with those two!'

'Bang on?' Damien protests. 'All you did was take the piss.'

'Well, if mine was anything to go by,' Jonny says, 'I did you both a favour.'

'Oh, you class act,' Damien charges. 'Freshly married and banging pissy slappers in nightclub loos.'

'Granted, the boat race was a bit off centre,' Jonny admits, 'but the chassis was tip top. See those *legs?!*'

'You're a married man now, you savage!'

Jonny drops himself at the pavement's edge, winding down into a post-conflict serenity.

'We've left our drinks in there, you cunt,' Damien realises aloud.

Evan produces a half-full glass from the inside of his beer-stained jacket. 'I've got mine.'

Damien grabs it. ''Ere, give us some!'

He passes round the smuggled-out glass, then throws the empty glass on to a grocer's rooftop.

Damien drops himself down next to Jonny. 'You alright?'

'I fuckin' lost. They even gave me the decision, and I still lost.'

Evan throws his arms up. 'It was a fucking *wrestling match*! There will be others. Trust me. Anyway, you didn't lose, they disqualified him— '

Jonny's up and running for a passing 159 bus.

'Whatcha doin'! 'Evan shouts. 'I'll give you a lift!'

Jonny makes the platform and is gone.

6. THE COFFEEVILLE PINCH

The first thing outsiders learn when coming to London is that there's London ... and there's *London*.

There's the London that Jonny lives in over in Notting Dale. Then there's that endless green suburban belt that fades out into the rest of England.

And there's the London he came down here for.

The holiest of holies.

The one he found here ... in Soho.

This London.

All this neon-noir attracts the lost ones from life's underbellies: from the peripherals of the straight world. Within reason, you can be anything you want here. Don't matter if you're rich, poor, black, white, queer, commie or even Welsh. No-one gives a fuck; all the freaks come here to gaze into each other's abyss. For Jonny, Soho is salvation in times of personal crisis, which, in the aftermath of tonight's assumed defeat at the hands of Kelly Hewitt, is why he comes here now.

Coffeeville is a coffee bar, and midnight is of the very recent past. The trebly out-of-tune guitar twang of *Angel Baby* by *Rosie and the Originals* plays on the jukebox. The drizzle on the window renders the world outside a Day-Glo Pollock abstract.

A greyed-out man in a shabby suit sits alone at the counter drinking espresso as if pencilled into this scene like an afterthought. A waitress is giving the red lacquered table tops the once-over with a cloth, exuding end-of-tether ennui. Three wired mohair-attired Mods sit around a table by the window, bug eyed and mouths on autopilot.

The open/closed sign on the door rattles as Jonny tries to enter, first pulling, then pushing, attracting a cursory glance from all within. He stumbles inside. His immaculate quiff and D.A are wrecked, and his shirt is rendered transparent by the rain. He almost slips on the gleaming tiles as he makes his way to the counter. He glances quickly at the Mods, but they fail to register this lapse of cool as they enter the fifth gear of their Dexy-fuelled chatter.

Finding no-one behind the counter, Jonny steadies himself against it and bangs loudly on its sugar-dashed surface. 'Milk!'

The startled waitress quickly appears and pours into a large glass from an oversized bottle.

Jonny eyes the bottle suspiciously. 'Is that red top?'

'What?'

'Is that red top?'

'No. Silver.'

'As long as it's not gold.'

He spots the bread rolls behind the glass display case. 'Gimmie one o' them. Cheese.'

'What happened to *please*?'

'*Cheese*, please.'

She places the food and drink before him.

Jonny smells his right hand before checking the state of his jaw again. The rain has made short work of any trace of that girl at the Locarno. He can speak, so his jaw's not broken, but it feels like he's been stabbed under the ear.

I fuckin' lost . . .

Tonight's failures are still eating him. A re-run of an old success might do the trick. He looks around the near empty bar then brings his unfocused gaze back to the waitress, who eyes him with cold contempt.

'Where's Brigitte? She still work here?'

'I don't know no Brigitte.'

'She was a dancer on Cool for Cats.'

Her blank countenance tells him she has no idea that he's talking about the TV show.

'Okay then.'

Jonny chances a bite of the cheese roll. His left nostril waterfalls blood, soaking it in nasal gore. He considers the bloodstained food in his hand. Fuck it. Waste not, want not. He jams the rest in his mouth and chews, painfully. He registers the waitress looking on, aghast. Jonny swallows, agonisingly slow, shrugs and tells her, 'It's all protein, right?'

At the other end of the counter, the greyed-out man gives Jonny a side-long appraisal, taking in the neat, powerfully sculptured torso. The tattoos on Jonny's arms depict a vicious battle between a panther and a giant python on one and a peacock on the other; *Les Skuse of Bristol* masterworks.

Oblivious to the appraisal, Jonny reaches into his pocket and slams a handful of outsized coins on the counter. He grins stupidly. 'Help yourself.'

The waitress, immune to displays of this type, sorts through the coins and takes the correct amount to the till.

The music stops.

The jukebox performs its mechanical selection.

Sharp, stabby guitars herald Gene Vincent's *Right Here on Earth*.

The loud ding of the till ruptures Gene's smooth rocker as Jonny knocks back a huge gulp of warm milk.

The greyed-out man says to the waitress, 'Another espresso please, dear.'

A whoosh, a gurgle and a lot of steam later, the greyed-out man nurses the frothy brew in front of him as he continues his appraisal of the rude newcomer.

'Excuse me, I couldn't help wondering. Are you a boxer?'

The question interrupts Jonny's second gulp of milk. He warily eyes the stranger. 'Why? D'ya wanna fight?'

The greyed-out man splutters and laughs into his cup and looks around sheepishly, as if shamefully caught out. 'Ooh, I'd be a very disappointing opponent for you, I'm afraid. Not much of a challenge at all.'

Jonny gives him the 'up and down', semi-disgusted, and finishes his milk. He jerks his head back, attempting to shake some sobriety into it.

I fuckin' lost...

The greyed-out man looks slyly around the bar and moves to the stool next to Jonny, eyeing his formidable biceps. 'I bet with those arms you could kill someone with one punch.'

Jonny ignores the statement. That piercing headache that had migrated so agreeably south at the Locarno has migrated north again.

'Gimme a coffee,' Jonny orders the waitress. 'You got any aspirin?'

The waitress stops folding napkins, makes the coffee, brings it over and pushes the sugar bowl towards him. 'I ain't got no aspirin.'

Jonny takes a moment to figure out what the sugar bowl is. 'I don't take sugar!'

The greyed-out man places a couple of coins on the counter. The waitress slides them into her palm. Still devouring Jonny's biceps, the man says, 'Y'know, Adolf Hitler used to take seven sugars in his coffee.'

Jonny is startled to find the man so close and reappraises him with his *not you again* scowl. 'So fuckin' what! How many does Elvis take?'

'I've really no idea.' A lexicon of dubious potential behind the man's manic glare recalibrates. 'I want you to hit me. I'll pay.'

The violent change of subject takes a few seconds to appreciate.

Jonny faces the man for the first time. He has small watery, pip-like eyes, and a down-turned mouth that, to Jonny's mind, belongs at the bottom of a pond. 'What?'

'I *said*... I want you to *hit* me. I want you to ... give me a fucking good hiding.' Desperation enters into it. 'I want you to really fucking lay me out!'

He bunches up his weak fists and stares past Jonny into some abyss, as if some terrible enemy is approaching.

'You're cracked. Piss off!'

The man's stare fixes itself back on Jonny. 'No *really*. I mean it. I'll pay. I'll give you ten pounds.'

'I said fuck off.'

'Fifteen then. I'll give you fifteen pounds.' He reaches inside his jacket pocket and waves the overlarge notes in Jonny's face.

Jonny and the greyed-out man face each other in a dark alleyway as a light drizzle moistens the scene. Jonny looks at the damp notes in his hand, pockets them and lunges forward, delivering a full crack across the man's jaw. The force of the blow turns him around and into the wall behind him with a wet smack, losing a shoe mid spin. He then slips on some soggy cardboard, which sends him sprawling to the rubbish-strewn cobblestone.

He fumbles with the front of his trousers and begins to masturbate. 'Oh, my God! Oh my God!'

Jonny hesitates over the gurgling weirdo and backs off, horrified, and out of the alley onto the street into a lamppost. He steadies himself against it and throws up into the gutter.

That gang of wired Mods exit Coffeeville. They see Jonny and cheer. They slap him on the back as they walk past, giving him the '*go on my son*' treatment. He can do nothing but heave again as they swagger off, laughing in their Dexy-fuelled hilarity.

The greyed-out man cries, 'I deserve it! Oh God, I deserve it!'

A firm hand comes out of nowhere and grabs Jonny by the scruff of his shirt, turns him around and slams him against a shop window which cracks on impact. Jonny swings blindly and hits his attacker, hard. He swings again, but his attacker dodges and drops him to the ground with a powerful blow to the stomach. Jonny looks up—a boot across his throat—to see a big police constable looming over him.

'Consider yourself pinched.'

7. THE SCRUBS

Prison.
　Actual... fucking... prison.
　HMP Wormwood Scrubs, no less.
Go directly to jail.
Do not pass go.
Do not collect fuck all.
Do not lip the screws.

You'll never see daylight again, so he'd been told by the hapless sap whose case was to be called after Jonny's.

He didn't mean to hit that copper. The silly cunt got in the way of a half-assed right-hook, meant for whoever was stupid enough to grab him by the collar and caught it in the teeth. The *whoever* being... a police constable. His helmet fell off into a puddle and bounced into the middle of the road. Made it worse somehow, the helmet falling off. Short-back-and-slap exposed to the Soho rain—much worse—made him look like a right cunt. Which is why Jonny thought it prudent to stay put once the boot was across his throat. Fair enough, a pinch was inevitable. But *actual* fucking prison?

Chokey?
The stripey hole?
Never in his wildest dreams...
What a day.

'*Plead guilty, and it'll go easier for you! It'll be a fine, a slap on the wrist, and we can all go home.*'

Jonny believed him, the desk sergeant, into whose grace and favour he was unceremoniously hauled at Holborn Police Station. A big fucker with an Oswald Mosley moustache and smelled of sweet tea, but seemed like a nice bloke. Wide, honest eyes held Jonny's gaze with an earnest, furrowed, sincere brow that bore the weight of a fair deal. The white painted brick walls that surrounded them offered a guaranteed abyss, a promise of a hard immovable future—the kind of tomorrow Jonny had no desire to be in.

No, he would take whatever deal was offered—the big fucker's fair deal—and avoid the void. Jonny was made to be seen, not buried in a hole.

Turned out Sergeant Fair-Deal was a lying, fucking toad. The Nazi moustache should have been a clue. What Jonny thought he'd be pleading to was affray for fighting. What the big dopey arresting officer was claiming was that he'd interrupted Jonny and another unidentified male *at it* in a public place and was attacked by Jonny when attempting to restore public decency. *At it* had only vague connotations for Jonny at the time, but he figured it meant something *poofy*. Unluckily for Jonny, the weirdo ran off, taking his corroborating account with him. Even less fortunate for Jonny was the small void in the copper's trap where a lateral incisor was meant to be. Assaulting a copper? This might have been considered the more serious offence, but Jonny would sooner take a thousand years for this than one second admitting to being a poof.

To cut to it: Jonny pled assault, and so off they sent him, for three weeks of remand, through ancient doorways, into rattling, Black Mariah vans, loud bolts, slamming doors, empty cells, naked queues, dimpled buttocks of the flabby queen in front of him, the unbearable proximity of exposed genitals behind him.

The sullen gang was led into a huge dorm. No cell. No solitary confinement. The smell of stale piss and perspiration completed those five dimensions of misery. An open concrete floor was flanked on either side by eight bunks against stone walls, painted white.

Someone down the line muttered, *'They don't mind a bit of white gloss, do they? The governor must have shares in Dulux.'*

Someone giggled.

Someone else shouted, *'I deny that emulsion for summary judgment!'*

A screw, standing by the door, screamed, *'Shut your fuckin' 'ole!'*

By now they had their clothes—standard-prison-issue—and carried them over and dropped them on their designated bunks. The screaming screw left the dorm. The group exchanged what-the-fuck glances, but before escape-plan fantasies could fully form, the screw was back, accompanied by another one with a clipboard who made a quick assessment of all present, if not entirely correct.

The screaming screw screamed again, *'As you are!'* and left. The other one sat at his desk, studying his clipboard.

The few prisoners who knew the drill sat on their bunks and immediately started pulling their trousers on, then putting their tin mugs and toothbrushes under the metal bunk-side tables. Jonny and the uninitiated followed suit.

The bloke on Jonny's left, nearest the end wall, came over.

'Hullo. I'm Freddy.'

Freddy had dirty blonde, tussled hair, which topped a long friendly face. You could almost call him good-looking if it wasn't for the broken nose and nicotine-stained teeth. Freddy had deep, hollow cheeks that Jonny assumed was the result of sucking one too many fags. Cigarettes: Jonny defined them as a flame on one end and an idiot on the other. Freddy's accent was pure born and bred saaarf Laaandon, whose caustic accent was somewhat dulled by the nasal muffle of that seriously twisted *Duke of Montrose,* which heralded his face like a caution.

Freddy filled Jonny in . . .

'Them two over there, they're queers. So don't be looking over there after lights-out, unless you like watching blokes gripping each other up.'

Jonny looked over at the so accused; just a couple of ordinary looking young blokes. Clearly, Freddie was having a giggle. Blokes would never do that.

'And I'd avoid the big wog by the door,' Freddie continued. 'Syphilis. Lousy with it. Going blind, so I'm told.'

Freddy then nodded towards the little ginger tough nut with the bum fluff in the opposite corner. 'Benjy Craddock. Little cunt. Too much to prove. He will come it, given half the chance. Give him an inch and he'll take the piss. Put him down at your first opportunity or you will forever have him in your face.'

Jonny glanced over at Benjy. Barely out of his teens: baby-faced, but something to be wary of behind those little piggy eyes—two tiny vacancies that promised a much bigger, colder, emptier one.

Benjy sensed Jonny and Freddy's scrutiny and returned it. Jonny had already perfected his ice-cold countenance and presented it accordingly. Benjy seemed to lose interest in his admirers and engaged in some admiration of his own— of the big grolly he'd raked out of his right nostril before putting it in his mouth.

That night, when the lights went out for the first time, Jonny lay there for hours in a black universe of shock.

How?

The fuck . . .

. . . has it come to this?

Those first few days were a blur. Jonny thought it prudent to get his head shaved in anticipation of any violent engagements. The currency for any service here was tobacco and Mars bars. So, one Mars Bar later had Jonny watching glumly as his crowning glory was sheared off into a pile on the floor, and swept into the corner with everyone else's.

He learned to play chess.

He was fed at least—breakfast, lunch and dinner. Made the most of the small exercise yard that the guards ushered them into for an hour a day, overlooked by the jeering prisoners—the proper ones—the over twenty-ones—who yelled obscenities and threats from their barred windows.

'What happened to your hair?'
'What's it look like? They shaved it off.'
How Jane got the good news was something of a mystery. But got it she did. On the seventh day, he was working out in the yard when they came and told him he had visitors. His heart stopped when the distinct possibility occurred of it being his father, or worse, his mother, or even worse . . . both.

On the other side of the glass, she sits with her brother Danny. She looked good at the best of times, pregnant as she was, but now, with a week's worth of raging testosterone devouring Jonny from the guts up, she is positively dick-warping.

In case of emergency, break glass.

Perhaps she had predicted his agony and tried to dress down in a loose cream sweater and coat which failed to conceal her bump, but it was no good. If Danny hadn't been there, he might have taken a chance with the steel chair he was sitting on and that bullet-proof glass. A sound beating and solitary confinement be damned!

Once the hair enquiry had been settled, he has to ask. 'How'd ya find out?'

'I went to see your landlady. She held your room for a week but reckons she had to let it go.'

The Holborn coppers had given him one phone call. The only person he could think of who even had a phone was Stefania. So, he called her, asked her to bring his wedding suit for the court case and tried to make a joke of it. *'Hold the sandwiches.'*

'What about my stuff?'

'What stuff?'

'My Lon of London T-shirts and my magazines?'

I dunno. I'll go and see her again. She wouldn't have thrown them out. She likes you.'

He gets the feeling she is watching him with a fraction of heightened attention when she delivers this line. No way could she be thinking what he thought she could be thinking. The odd friendly dick-squeeze aside, the woman was old enough to have handed out programs at the crucifixion.

Danny cut in before Jonny's cool countenance could fail him. 'So when you gettin' out then, Jonny?'

'Got a court date in two weeks. How that pans out will dictate what happens after that. Remand is basically purgatory. Could go either way.'

Jane's full pink lip-sticked mouth wouldn't quit. Maybe it was just as well Danny is here. Jonny could end up doing something that would get him even more jail time.

'What's it like, prison?' Danny asks, in all teenage innocence.

Jonny answers, but his eyes stay on his oh so near and yet oh so far away wife.

'It's like school for bigger and even more deranged kids.'

The rest of the visit covers day-to-day family minutiae, who did what, who's started going out with who, and so on. Jonny would like to think that Jane's condition, and how she was getting on *downstairs,* was foremost in his mind, and it was certainly up there. As far as he could make out, she was taking to impending motherhood like a duck to water, but the gargantuan sex-elephant in the corner continued to dominate the whole hour and Jonny could think of nothing but getting on her.

Finally, the visit comes to an end, and they are told to go. Jonny calls Jane back.

'It's okay, Danny,' Jane tells her brother. 'I'll catch you up.'

She comes back to the window. 'What?'

'Show us your tits,' Jonny hisses. 'Quick!'

She sympathises. She really does. She gives a quick glance at the neighbouring cubicles, can see no-one, but that doesn't mean someone won't walk in just at the wrong moment.

'Show us your cock.'

Jonny glances around furtively and makes to reach into the front of his trousers. 'Okay, but tits first.'

'I'm joking! What are you doin'?!'

'What then?!'

'Just . . . I dunno! Just wait. I'll make it up to you.'

'Send a picture then.'

'How the fuck am I gonna get a picture? Who's gonna take it?'

'I dunno. Get one with one o' them timer things.'

'From who? And get it developed where?'

'Well, write me a fucking letter then. You know . . . about what you wanna do when I get out.'

'*If* you get out.'

'Fuck off!'

'They'll censor it, anyway. They read 'em, all your letters.'

'Just . . . fucking send something!'

'I love you Jonny. Hope you get out before the baby comes.'

This helps re-calibrate Jonny's priorities.

'And you,' he whispers.

A guard comes in to make sure everyone has left. He ushers Jane from the otherwise empty room to the door. Jonny watches her go with agonised longing. As the guard with his back turned straightens a few chairs, Jane liberates her breasts from her bra under her baggy jumper and lifts it up over her swollen belly in a lightning-quick, but delicious display of female flesh. Jonny didn't believe in God, but his atheism faltered in that microsecond. That microsecond of luscious, round, firm, pink, mind-blowing tits would serve him for weeks.

A surreptitious wank in a dorm full of other men is difficult, but not impossible. His wife's last-minute show of daring and, let's face it, generosity, might just see him through. She would have no idea just how badly he needed her now. A little of *her* daring would help *him* go a long way.

'Keep your head down, do as you're fucking told, and you'll be out of here before you can slap a copper in Soho,' Freddy japed.

That Benjy cunt seemed to avoid him. Which was just as well as Jonny didn't trust his ability to back down should push-come-to-pulverise, sex deprivation or no sex deprivation. He just told himself to eat whatever bullshit these fuckers ladle out, and he would catch up with them on the outside should the need and occasion ever present itself.

He was a bona fide jailbird now. Despite this, *she came to see him*. Found him and came to see him. Most birds would turn their back if their bloke got put away.

Okay.

Take stock.

He would play a straight game now.

Get out.

Get his mission back on track.

Get a place before the baby arrives.

Fuck those Acton bolt factory housewives.

Fuck *Cool for Cats* Brenda.

And fuck pissy slappers in nightclub shitters.

Straight game now.

That next Saturday afternoon, everyone from the dorm is playing football in the yard to the usual jeers of the real prisoners—spitting and throwing garbage on their game. The perfect time for a shower.

Jonny has his soap and his towel and heads for the bathhouse. Someone is in there. He can hear the heavy pressure of water splashing on concrete in one of the stalls.

When Jonny enters, Benjy is face and hands against the wall, and the *'big wog'* is going at him from behind. Jonny thinks they're in the middle of a fight. Then he sees . . . He didn't know you could even get it in there—never even considered the possibility. Why are they doing this?

Benjy turns his head, water smashing off his red hair in a crown of exploding water, and sees Jonny standing there. Benjy calls to him, 'C'mere!'

Jonny staggers back as if punched. He does a fast about-face and marches back to the dorm in a state of . . . he knows not what. A penny drops as he drifts down that dank corridor, followed by an entire bank vault. The poofs he's known—the ones that tried to cop a feel during those Belgravia bodybuilding photoshoots—th*is* is what they were after? This is what they did?!

Until this moment, Jonny thought poofs and queers were just funny blokes that acted like girls. The idea that they did anything sexual was like an H-Bomb going off in his face. It was so obvious now, but until four minutes ago there'd been an entire world that was hidden from him, that has now revealed itself.

The blackie's syphilis occurred. Even if you wanted to do something like that, why would you do it with someone with the clap? Can men even catch the clap from each other? Maybe it was a lie.

Even so . . . *Why?*

Jonny was all about learning, expanding, and embracing the world and all the madness it has to offer.

But this?

Jonny is a jailbird Icarus.

The birdman of Wormwood Scrubs.

Today, he's reached a little too high.

He's seen a little too much.

The next two weeks couldn't pass fast enough now that sodomy was no longer just the stuff of Biblical fairy tales. Attuned to the potential of the threat of such activity, the hours drag agonisingly until finally the day is upon him.

He is bench pressing heavy weights in the busy prison gymnasium when a guard steps into the room.

'Come in number 331012, your time is up!'

Jonny reluctantly replaces the bar. The reluctance momentarily frightens him. Three weeks and he was institutionalised already?

The guard clocks it. 'If I didn't know better, I'd think you were sorry to leave us, Mr Arnold.'

Jonny's return to the courtroom was a mercifully hurried and ultimately sweet affair. They were letting him go. £30 court costs to be paid in weekly instalments.

'Miss one week and you'll be back inside!' says the be-wigged and ruddy-faced judge.

Luckily, he still had the fifteen quid that that Coffeeville freak had given him. Jonny had no idea how he'd raise the other fifteen, but he'd worry about that (and no doubt a few other things) once he was out.

When they first brought him in, it was in a Black Mariah van that took him to a yard in the back somewhere. Today, once they got him back to jail from the courtroom to get his stuff, they let him out the front. They unlock the big steel and heavy oak door and pull it in. From across Du Cane Road, it looks like a piece being pushed out of a jigsaw puzzle.

He steps out into a warm but overcast afternoon and feels something of a tool as he stands there in his wedding suit, in his Cornflakes-box-emboldened shoes, with his holdall under his arm, beneath the front edifice of Her Majesty's Wormwood Scrubs Prison, with its plaster reliefs of famous reformers whose names Jonny has no care to remember.

He is free again.

The concept momentarily confuses him. He is still in shock over getting put away in the first place. He knows, somehow, that he will carry a little of it around with him forever.

An ex-Jailbird.

Forever.

He walks down the driveway, back to the world, a world he is fixed on staying in.

Jane said she was going to meet him. But he wouldn't—*couldn't*—blame her, if she didn't. Maybe the enormity of the situation got to her.

He scans the busy high street and waits . . . and waits. He is entering some kind of trance when she hops off a bus on the other side of the road. She is in a maroon blazer and a tweed skirt. Her hair is piled high into an immaculate black ozone-destroying beehive hairdo. Her eyes are rendered bat wings by the heavy black mascara. That swollen abdomen is now very much in evidence.

He put his hand on her belly.

They melt in each other's regard.

This moment will never happen again.

Neither of them wants to end it.

'I want to kiss you,' he says.

'What's stopping you?'

'I can't kiss you *and* look at you.'

8. CINECETTA CALLING!

'Hey kid, where do you work out?'
'The Forester's Club.'

From the hole he is digging on the North side of Bayswater Road, Jonny gives the man with the American accent a quick up and down. That ice-blue Bugs Moran suit barely contained a frame that was at least 6.5 and touching 300lbs. This mid-afternoon visage is topped by heavy dark glasses and a trim beard. The man is tanned, and it has to be said, good-looking.

Jonny has to ask. 'You a wrestler?'

'On occasion, but I'm in movies now. I'm just taking a break between films and doing a bit of talent scouting for a casting director. Do you know 'Tiger' Joe Robinson?'

Jonny kind of does and says so. 'Not personally, but I know who you mean. He used to be a wrestler. He did that film, *A Kid for two Farthings* with Primo Carnera and Diana Dors.'

'That's him. Well, Tiger Joe's in Rome now and doing great. You know you would do great out there too. They'd give you work, no problem. You're in much better shape than Robinson, and he's making serious bread.'

'Serious bread?'

'Huh?'

'What's *serious* bread?'

'Money, honey. Lots of it.' The big man chuckles. 'Sorry, kid—an Americanism. Took you limeys a thousand years to invent the English language and a coupla hundred for us Yanks to fuck it all up.'

The big man's chuckle gears down into a chortle. 'But seriously, come see me.'

He reaches into his big jacket and pulls out his wallet. It looks like snakeskin . . . shiny red and green scales . . . The big man flips out a card and hands it down. 'I'm Jerry. Jerry Pro.'

Jonny studies the card and sees the words—*Jeremy Prokievich – Ufficio Produzione Cinecittà*—printed in embossed gold copperplate on a matt black card.

Jonny makes to hand it back.

'No,' Jerry Pro says. 'Keep it. There's my address right there. Come see me and I'll give you the low-down. I got an apartment just up the way there.'

Jerry Pro makes a two-handed frame with his fingers and one-eyes Jonny, still standing in his hole, through it. 'I kid thee not, kid, you'll be a smash in pictures.'

Jonny is working for Turriff's now, who are contracted to the Water Board. It was one of the fellas from the Foresters gym who pointed him in Turriff's direction. They were desperate for people and Jonny was a desperate person, so now he's digging roads and fixing leaks in the West End.

On his release from jail, Jonny's desperation forced him to consider joining the army. But his internal mantra of being made to be seen wouldn't work with camouflage.

No. Not one little bit.

For the first few nights after getting out, he slept on benches in the park, in view of the very prison he'd just been released from. But with this *real* job, and a few matches for DeMarto's Wresting promotions, he scraped enough together to move back in to his old Notting Dale bedsit with Stefania. As soon as she knew he was out of jail, she cast the smack-off who took his room out into the West Ken wilderness from whence he came.

Jane never did go back to her old job. Now, she was helping her mum's seamstress work, making dresses and suits and dropping them off around the neighbourhood. They were still a long way off from being able to even afford a deposit to rent a flat. At the current rate, Jane will still be living at home when the baby arrives. Talk about doing everything arse upwards ...

Jonny has been on this road all week. The sun's out so he's got his shirt off for an uneven tan. His Tony Curtis quiff is growing back. He is becoming whole again.

He gets stared at, by blokes for the most part. If it's birds, it's only when there's a group of them, whispering and giggling as they hurry past. Once, one of them, bolder than her chums, shouted back, 'Can I have a feel to see if it's real!'

But, for the most part, it's blokes, staring at him from across the road, or the nearest bus stop, or the park behind the fence. Sometimes they were nowhere to be seen, but he could sense them. He could feel them in the vicinity. Roach legs of repulsion crawled up his back as memories of that Coffeeville freak comes back to him, and Benjy and that clap-ridden blackie in The Scrubs. But what can he do? What did *they* think he was going to do? He used to scowl at them, but now, fuck it, let 'em gawp. One day, everyone will be looking at him. Better get used to it.

But, when Jerry Pro appeared seemingly from nowhere and blocked out the late afternoon sun, Jonny felt instinctively that the man's intentions were honourable. He didn't scuttle about in Jonny's peripheral vision like an insect. He came straight up and stated his case, like men do. Jonny slips the card in the back pocket of his jeans.

'What's your name, kid?'

'Jonny. Kid "Tarzan" Jonathan in the ring.'

'Oh, so *you're* a wrestler!'

'Well,' Jonny looks up the road, wipes his nose and spears the shovel into the dirt. 'On occasion. When I'm not doing this.'

'Hey, we all gotta earn till our ship comes in, right?'

Jonny detects a sympathetic glimmer behind the big man's sunglasses.

'When you finish today, come see me.'

Jonny watches Jerry Pro's—'*I'm-all-the-world*'—swagger towards Marble Arch.

That big dispute at Hammerstone's comes to him—about acting — about being the next Troy Donahue. He'd come to London to be a wrestler, not a fucking actor. Can it be that easy? Like an Elvis film? One minute: surly, reluctant shit-kicker—next: King of Rock 'n' Roll. Would being an actor harm or enhance his chances of being the greatest wrestler the world has ever seen?

Chances?

What fucking chances?

He blew the only one he had with Hammerstone's and no-one else was laying siege to his door. He hardly had a door to lay siege to!

Fuck it. Go see the bloke.

A faint heart never fucked a pig.

At 5pm he downs tools, tells the foreman 'Ta lah', grabs his shirt and makes his way up Bayswater high street.

As the bloke said, it's only ten minutes' walk from where he'd been working all day, up by those flats where Jack Spot the gangster and his missus got a serious twatting from his rival Billy Hill and his mob a few years back.

He comes to a red-bricked Georgian block of flats. He rings the bell; the bell rings back, and he hears the door unlock.

He climbs an ornate spiral of carpeted stairs. When Jerry Pro answers the door in a short silk dressing gown, Jonny's heart sinks and thinks maybe this bloke is some kind of queer after all. The man beckons him in.

With no small amount of relief, the first thing Jonny sees through an open bedroom door is a naked woman, seemingly asleep, laying across a huge four-poster bed. The golden mounds of her perfect bum mesmerises him as he stands hesitantly in the hallway.

Jerry Pro chuckles and says, 'Give me a minute. Go out on the balcony. I'll be right out.'

Jonny goes to where the man directs him and crosses a vast suite of expensive furniture and plush drapes to get there. The balcony overlooks Hyde Park near where he has been digging all day. The traffic below is heavy, and he watches the tops of the buses as they make their slow progress up and down the high street. From inside, he hears the slow moans of the woman from the bedroom and Jerry Pro's shushing her. The moans stop abruptly, and Jonny assumes the man had put his hand over her mouth. He is about to sit on one of the small wrought-iron seats when the man appears, tying up his silken robe, still chuckling.

'Sorry about that. Unfinished business. Wanna beer?'

The man looks like a star. Tall. Tanned. Toned. All these Americans do. The bodybuilders down at the Foresters, the GIs that came over during the war, they were born stars. And now, here is Jonny talking to one about being one himself.

Jerry comes back with a couple of unchilled bottles of Double Diamond.

They sit and sip.

A flock of pigeons arise in a flurry and seem to dissolve into the afternoon sun.

Jerry Pro fills him in. 'You'll fly out to Rome. You flown before?'

'No.'

'You'll go for it. From up there you'll realise this world 'ain't so big.'

'How much is that gonna cost, though?'

'They'll reimburse you. Don't worry about any o' that.'

Jonny will have to front this thing? There's a red flag right there.

Jerry writes an address on a headed notepad, tears off the page, and hands it over. 'Give 'em this—it's the production office address—to any taxi driver and they'll know where to go. When you get there, they'll reimburse you the taxi fare too.'

Jonny studies the note.

TUSCOLINA, ROMA, ITALIA . . .

'And in the meantime, I'll phone the casting director and tell him to expect you.'

Jerry Pro goes into a dizzying spiel of Italiano film-lore which, for the most part, goes straight over Jonny's head. Steve Reeves, Reg Parks and the aforementioned Tiger-Joe are all familiar names, who have all by now achieved an obscure kind of stardom. Reeves had kicked off the current Sword and Sandals craze which saw no sign of abating, but when the chitty chat segues to the directors, Cubucci . . . Parolini . . . Campagaliani et al.? Forget it.

As Jerry Pro's wise-up continues, Jonny tries to see himself going toe to toe with Reeves in a Hercules sequel. The idea is not that hard to imagine.

'I love those films. Just saw Ulysses Against the Son of Hercules at the Rialto last week.'

'Yeah, Mike Lane. You know he's over two meters tall? A monster, the guy.'

Jonny's heart sinks. His being way under six feet might be a factor. 'I'm 5.9,' Jonny exaggerates.

'Relax.' Jerry Pro sips from his bottle while keeping one eye on Jonny's perfectly proportioned visage. He puts the bottle on the floor and does that two-handed frame thing with his fingers again and looks at Jonny through it. 'A low camera angle can put feet on you. Besides, they can't all be giants, otherwise none of them will look it. No, I can see you as a David/underdog type. In fact, that's it! David and Goliath! I'll tell 'em. You got Michelangelo's David writ all over ya.'

Jonny does as he is told. He relaxes. The logic holds. He can see it. They can't all be giants . . .

'You got a passport?'

The question breaks the spell and drags Jonny off Mount Olympus, deflecting lightning-bolts, and back onto this Bayswater balcony holding a warm beer. 'No.'

'Well, you'll need one.' The man stands up, signifying the meeting is over. Talent isn't going to scout itself. Besides, with the girl with the golden arse in the other room, Jonny would hate to keep Jerry Pro from it.

The man walks him to the door and ushers him out. 'Don't leave it too long.'

'I've never even done acting before.'

'You've seen those movies, right? You just need to look good. Let the directors worry about your acting.' Jerry Pro's firm handshake is warm and dry. 'Nice to meet you, Jonny. Don't leave it too long.'

'Thanks. I won't.'

By the time he gets to his bedsit, Jonny thinks he's figured out a way to play this bitter, but very, *very*, sweet turn of events as regards Jane.

He remembers *Hercules vs. the Hydra* is on a rerun at the Bughole—the old cinema on Portobello Road—with the Hungarian bodybuilder Micky Hargitay as the bearded one.

So, he will call her.

They will go out on a date.

He will take her to see said film.

He will put it to her. *Can you imagine me in one of those films?*

She will respond positively, and he will spring this very real possibility upon her—give her the same spiel as Jerry Pro had given him, dazzle her with his newfound intel on Italian directors, tell her about the thousands he will surely be making before the year's out . . . I mean, that's what they get, right? Thousands?

She will be astounded.

She will be thrilled.

She will be married to a film star.

He can use his film star fame to relaunch his siege on the wrestling world.

The only thing he hasn't factored in . . . is Jayne Mansfield.

Hercules vs. the Hydra looks like it cost about four quid to make, but Jonny sees himself in every scene—killing a raging bull with his outsized sword and besting the Hydra with a triple beheading of the three-headed beast. But as soon as Big Jayne explodes onto the screen, vamping it up and spilling out of her toga and, seemingly, the screen itself, Jonny knows he's mis-stepped.

The film ends, and Jane holds it down until they duck into the nearest pub. Knowing Big Jayne has already blown his plan of attack, he charges in anyway, with all the ambrosia and honey that bigshot Jerry Pro had poured upon him.

None of it has the same effect on Jane.

'You ain't going to no fuckin' Italy!'

'It's a couple of *weeks*! A month, tops!'

'So, while I'm here having your baby, you're out there shaggin' Gina Lob-a-brick-at-her, or whatever her fuckin' name is!'

'Look at me, I'm digging fucking roads. How am I supposed to support a family with what Turriff's are paying?'

'And how are you supposed to support a family if you're on the other side of the world?'

'I'll be making money! Some *real* money! Thousands!'

'So, what happened to the wrestling then? It's all you bin goin' on about ever since I've known yer, and now you're gonna be a film star?!'

I *am* gonna be a wrestler! I *am* a wrestler! Jane, I've been down here five years, going round and round in circles, finally got a shot and fucked it. I just gotta find another way in.'

By now, their raised voices attract the attention of the rest of the pub. Jonny thinks of wising her up to the term *serious bread*, but instinct tells him this will confirm that there is already distance between them, that he is already on the other side of the world.

You ain't going to no fucking Italy!

No-one, not even his new wife, tells Jonny what to do. This is exactly the sort of order that will have him hailing a taxi and heading straight for the airport—lack of passport notwithstanding.

But no.

He takes a deep, discrete breath, heralds in a new era of maturity, and dials it down.

'Jane. You trust me, *right?*'

She shifts position while keeping her eyes on his. She softens, considers, but comes to the same conclusion. 'No, I fucking don't. If a bird puts it on a plate, no bloke is gonna turn it down, is he?'

'Why do you think I married you? I'm in this for the long haul.'

'Cos I'm pregnant, that's why.'

'What difference does *that* make? Loads of blokes get a bird knocked up and take it on the toes. I ain't one of them and you know it.'

Jane scans the room, facing down all and any scrutiny. The curious go back to their own business—to their own drinks. She looks towards the bar—at the seemingly carefree men and women still jousting, still carousing in the era of the day's mating rituals. An era now lost to her. And then she looks at Jonny. 'If you go, we're finished.'

That *heart* Jonny has: some of it falls out of him now because he knows himself and he knows that he always deals with immovable obstacles with unstoppable force. Jane's defiance—her *childish* defiance—makes it real. He knows now that he *is* going to Italy to be a film star. Her ultimatum seals it. Already, as she watches his eyes, waiting for his response, his mind has already fast-forwarded to the part where he goes to the embassy to get his passport, the travel place on Latimer Road where he will buy his ticket, flying over the Channel and being up where the Luftwaffe got fucked by Spitfires . . . touching down in a land of legends . . . basking in a sun that had shone on emperors and gladiators . . . a series of exciting firsts . . .

He's already there.

It's already happening.

The harsh jang-a-lang-a-clang of the bell's last orders snaps him right back to this pub where he has much to catch up on.

He wonders when he last cried.

Then his insides turn to granite and he says simply, 'Then we're finished.'

9. A TALE OF TWO DADDIES

Jonny flung his head back to avoid the full impact of the blow, but not enough to take a fraction off of what could have been with his chin. Jonny caught his father's wrist and spun him around, where he tripped backwards and fell conveniently onto the chair. The man grabbed the saucepan and sprung back at him, brandishing it high above his head in a killer-blow fashion. Jonny crouched and launched himself at his father's stomach and managed to flip him over. The old man's flight was abruptly halted as he hit the wall upside down. Two feet higher and he would have gone through the window.

Eamon Arnold conceded the round and struggled ignobly to right himself on the floor. Gasping heavily, he sat back against the wall and considered, with a wry eye, his son standing over him. 'That it? What else you got?'

'What else do I need?' Jonny challenged. 'You're on the deck and I'm still standing.'

This attack from his father came as no surprise. The only thing surprising about it was that it had taken all day to come about.

As soon as Jonny downed tools that Friday, he hit Clarkson's travel place and discovered that air tickets, a la Air Alitalia, were way and above anything he could scrape together in good time. Alternative modes of travel would have to be considered. Boat? Bus? Hitchhike? But whatever the case, this enterprise cannot happen without hard cash. Fast.

Jonny had the whole weekend mapped out.

Tonight: reps, 500 press-ups; 500 sit-ups; 500 curls; the seven o'clock showing of *Cleopatra* at the Bughole; a wank before bedtime (hopefully with inspiration from big tits across the way); Forester's gym in the morning, see if anyone wants a pull around, use their phone and call DeMarto's for some matches to raise travel funds . . . all while figuring out a way to re-sell this Italian adventure to Jane. She *has* to come around. The baby will be here any day now. She has no choice.

So, the last thing he needed after digging roads all week and begin a meticulously planned weekend was coming home to the very reason he left home in the first place.

He'd only just got in when Stefania calls up the stairs that someone is here for him. This was not usual. The first thing that goes through his head is that maybe this is some kind of follow up to his jail time. He isn't on probation, but who knows how the long arm works? Once you've made a pact with those devils—incurred the wrath of the big blue— maybe they're on you for eternity, ready to pounce on the first slip up.

Had he slipped up?

But then hope makes an entrance . . . *Jane*!

Total radio silence had ensued since their showdown the other week. She must be just about ready to drop now. There's no way she would go through with it all without him.

He knew she'd weaken.

Got to be her . . .

The heavy-footed clumping coming up the stairs vetoed this hope. Stefania yells after the visitor, *'First on ze left!'*

The first option re-establishes itself.

The authorities.

That long arm . . .

Jonny makes a quick appraisal of the room. The girlie mags are safely under the mattress. He has nothing else to hide. He listens at the door. The silence does what silence did. It tells him nothing.

He opens it . . . to the same disappointment he felt when he first clapped eyes on his father, still in uniform, getting off the train after the war. The unbelievable quickly becomes the believable.

'What do *you* want?'

'Nice, that is. Nice welcome.'

'Well, you're not. Welcome. What do you want?'

'I've come to see *you*, you daft sod.'

Jonny makes a quick scan of the vacant hallway behind the man as he stands at his door.

'Had a row with Mam, have you?'

Eamon Arnold won't bless this accuracy with an answer when a sneer will suffice. So, sneer he does.

Satisfied the man is unaccompanied, Jonny bids him in. Eamon drops his case in the middle of the floor, casts his eyes around the room then fixes them on his son.

'And you left home for *this*?'

'I left home to be a wrestler. And to get away from you.'

'Oh yeah, a *wrestler*,' he snorted. 'And how's that coming on, then?'

'A lot better than my getting away from you, it seems. How did you find me?'

'Oh, Paulie's mother.'

Ah . . . Paulie Ingram . . . Jonny's old school chum who had been promising to come down until that bout of Polio took the wind out of his sails.

Eamon moves his case aside with his foot and goes over to the window. 'Does that kettle work?'

'Yeah, it works.'

Jonny fills it and puts it on the stove. He leans back against the only available wall and assesses his father as he peers out into the yard. The greying hair was recently cut—regulation short-back-and-sides. It's how he had it as an infant. It's how he had it in the army. It's how he still has it in the pit. It's how he will have it in his box.

A navy one-button gabardine jacket, tanned slacks and heavy, well-worn brown leather shoes. Jonny tries to follow the man's eye line. What a hoot it will be if ol' big tits is doing her routine. How would that sit with daddy's puritan sensibilities?

It's only when his father turns around that Jonny registers the loose shirt with no tie and two—*count 'em—two* top buttons undone. This man has cut loose and is *spinning wild!* Out of Mam's orbit. Jonny would bet dollars to doughnuts that that tie is safely ensconced in that case of his and will be present and correct by the time he gets back home.

Jonny eyes the case under the table. A frightening realisation interrupts the appraisal.

'Where are you staying?'

'Oh, I thought I could stay here with you.'

FUCK!

'Dad, look around. The place sleeps one. Besides, the landlady wouldn't have it.'

'The landlady . . .' Eamon crinkles his nose disdainfully and lowers his voice. 'What is she, Russian, that woman?'

'Czech.'

The word seems to confuse the old man.

'Oslovakian.'

Eamon nods affirmation. A supposition confirmed. 'It's all communist though, innit?'

'Is it? She's also a Catholic, so you'll *love* her.'

'Pah! What a deluded bunch *they* are—'

'But anyway, you can't stay here.'

Eamon assesses the bed. 'We can top and turn. There's plenty of room if we top and turn.'

'*Dad*. She won't have it. She won't even let me have girls up here.'

Eamon slyly eyes the array of fleshy swim-suited models on the wall. Jonny's jail experience compelled him to remove the body-builders and wrestling heroes. He was now tuned into the possibility that if anyone saw half-naked men on his walls, they might think he was a bit . . . *like that*.

'*Girls* . . . it's hardly the same thing. I'm sure you can talk her round.'

'Even if I could, I'm not spending the night with your big cheesy trotters in my face.'

'What about *your* big cheesy trotters?!'

'It's *my* bed!'

Another frightening jolt.

'How long you expecting to stay?'

'Oh . . . well, a few days at least.'

'No way. I might be able to swing a night, but that's it. I'll sleep on the chair.'

'You can't sleep on the—'

'Anyway, what are you gonna do with a few days?'

'I dunno. Thought you could show me the sights, introduce me to all your friends.'

So *that* was it. Jonny's friend manifest was meagre. Daddy was here to report back to all those dolts in the pit, all those zealots at chapel, and all his dopey old school chums of how Jonny's siege on the capital and all his talk of making it big in wrestling had come to this, a doss house in Notting Dale with a box of porridge, five tea bags in the tin and a bottle of milk on the windowsill.

Fuck.

If only he had a match this weekend. Just one match . . . he could show him.

Eamon drops himself on the edge of the bed. 'Seriously, son. How are you making a living?'

Jonny could tell him about the Turriff's job, but shuddered at the thought of his dad taking that nugget back home. *The boy's diggin' roads!*

'I told you. Wrestling. For the independents, mainly. You caught me at the right time. I got nothing on this weekend.'

'So, it's not regular then?'

'No. But what is? Your beloved pit could collapse on you any day. Or your chapel.'

Eamon throws his son a fiery glance. Jonny knows better than to go down that road. They have been down it so many times before.

The kettle comes to a boil. Jonny takes it off and pours.

'Still two sugars, is it?'

Jonny hands over the tea. Eamon considers the mug like it's a poisoned chalice. 'Any of it go to the church? The money you make?'

'Oh yeah, sure. After every match, I throw my money up in the air and anything God wants, he keeps.'

The eye-fire returns. Jonny needs to change the subject and remembers . . . 'Oh, and I'm going to Italy. I'm gonna be in the flickers.'

Eamon's look of utter disbelief tells Jonny this is a truth too far. He hardly believed it himself, so what chance would the old man have? And then he remembers something else. He would have to keep the old man away from anyone who might spill about the jail time.

Who knew?

Jane and her brother.

Luckily, he wasn't expecting to see them anytime soon . . .

FUCK!

STEFANIA.

AND JANE!

MARRIED!

Outside of Jane's family, only Stefania and Paulie knew he had got married and that he was hurtling towards fatherhood. He would have to keep daddy from entering into any polite conversation with the landlady. He would have to get him out of here and somewhere he was unlikely to run into said meagre acquaintants.

'C'mon, you. We're going out.'

The museums are a cheap day out. Free, in fact. So the British Museum it is.

The 31-bus heads east, and despite himself, Jonny wants to know how Brynmawr is doing without him. They sit in silence together on the top deck, overlooking the early evening hustle and bustle of Shepard's Bush. The conductor winds off their tickets from the big metal contraption that hangs from his neck to his stomach and moves on to collect other fares. Jonny watches the back of the man as he goes down the bus—at his narrow shoulders, barely filing the faded black uniform that seems to wear him rather than the other way around. Those shoulders: abject dejection. When Jonny was growing up, he would wonder why people became bus drivers or conductors or, like his father, work in the coal mines. In his innocence, he assumed everyone did what they wanted to do. Why else would they be what they were? It didn't take long to understand that people did what they must. That most never had a choice. Most never seemed to *want* a choice. Not for Jonny. Jonny wanted options but saw nothing on his menu that was even worth wanting. Until, that is, when Paulie Ingram introduced him to his destiny and took him to that Assirati/Hessel match at Stowe Hill Baths Hall in Newport.

'How's Paulie?' Jonny ventures. 'Is he completely over the Polio now?'

The bus is passing Wormwood Scrubs when his father looks at him gravely before answering. For a moment, Jonny has the feeling that somehow the old man had heard of his recent incarceration and is now about to confront him with it. The next words that come out of Eamon's mouth made Jonny wished that *that* was all it is.

'Oh, hadn't you heard? He died.'

Jonny thought he'd heard wrong. His cognition seems to stutter and jam, creating a split-second blackout. Those spotlights that hung high above him as he lay flat on his back on the mat of the Lewisham Concert Hall after Hewitt's onslaught came to him now. He was right back there—dazzled by those Elysian quasars. The lights faded and were replaced by the face of his father, watching him with concerned interest, like you'd watch a cat encountering its reflection in a mirror for the first time.

'Did you hear what I said?'

Jonny's mouth comes to the rescue while his drowning mind scrambles for driftwood.

'He died? The letter said he was getting better. He sent a letter . . . Are you sure?'

'As sure as hitting a lamppost at sixty mile an hour.'

This statement collects the disparate parts Jonny is in and pulls him together.

'He had Polio. What do you mean?'

'That bloody bike of his . . . showing off in front of a couple of girls outside the Beaufort Ballroom. Got flung off and hit a lamppost. Died the next day. You didn't know?'

Jonny and God had never seen eye to eye—especially with how they'd been introduced by his fervent father—but this really sealed the deal. Of course, he never went for all that pie-in-in-the-sky bollocks he'd been pummelled with since he was old enough to believe in boogeymen, but when he got that letter shortly after coming down here, telling of how Paulie had contracted Polio, and that his chances were slim, Jonny flung himself down by the side of his bunk and prayed—prayed like a rabid believer that his friend would be alright. In his shock, he had no idea if he was praying to God exactly: just whatever benevolence there was in this existence—anything that would right this wrong.

It seemed that whatever it was had ears.

A month later, Jonny received the letter that said the worst was over and that Paulie was expected to make a full recovery. The last word he had from his old friend was that he'd just bought a motorbike and that he was planning on riding down to see him as soon as he'd gotten some cash together. Like all rational minds, Jonny was forced to accept coincidence and luck as the culprit. But whether it was God, chance, luck, destiny or fate that brought Paulie back from the brink, he was grateful to it.

And now this.

It explained the wedding no-show.

Jonny refuses to sully Paulie's memory by discussing this shocker with his father, so dismisses it with a vague, 'That bloody bike. I told him.' Jonny changes the subject, fast. 'So, how's Mam? How's everyone?' Jonny attempts a note of levity. 'You haven't told me anything about how they're all surviving without me.'

Eamon, momentarily taken aback by this unexpected tangent, gives Jonny a rundown of how Trevor, his older brother, had gotten into yet another one of his legendary punch ups with the gypsies over in Abergavenny; how Paulette, his little sister, had got a job in the chemists; how Mam was still having trouble with her knees, and how she was just using that as an excuse not to attend chapel . . . All this seems to drone on in the far-off distance as the reality of a world without Paulie Ingram cripples Jonny's universe. The last time he saw Paulie was at the train station, standing next to his mother, waving him off. It was early on a freezing Tuesday morning; his father would have been at work. Not that he would have been there, anyway. A controlled rage ascends now as his father sits beside him on this slow-moving bus. Jonny will have to visit home eventually, hopefully before anyone else dies, but not until he can return as a conquering hero, and not with his tail between his legs, desperately missing Mam's cooking. The death of Paulie Ingram reminds him that the clock is ticking, and that no death stops the world.

The Jonny Arnold who hops off the platform of this bus across the road from the museum is not the same Jonny Arnold who hopped on. To ponder the cruel fate of his dead friend in the presence of his father seems wrong in a way that Jonny cannot fathom. He will put it out of his mind until the old man is out of his face.

The Elgin Marbles are a thing to behold. Jonny has been to this museum many times before having, as he had, many rainy hours to kill over the last half-decade. The uncomfortable notion that these marvels have been more or less stolen from their place of origin does little to flatten Jonny's enjoyment of them. The chances of going to Greece any time soon are non-existent, so he is happy that the mountain has been brought to Mohammed, or in this instance, the Marbles to Jonny.

Of course, Eamon has to bring up the obvious.

'Terrible ... terrible ...'

'What is?'

'This!' Eamon gestures dismissively at the fractured 70-foot-wide marble freeze before them. 'It's vandalism, bringing them here.'

Jonny knows where this is going and gets there first. 'The Italians and the Turks had already blown these things to pieces. If they'd left them where they were, someone else would have destroyed the rest and they'd be nothing left of them at all.'

'Maybe that would have happened—maybe not. The point is, they had no right to steal them and keep them here.'

Jonny folds his arms as if to seal the subject shut. 'Well, I'm glad they did.'

But If Jonny has to put a starting point on where the day really began to deteriorate; it was when they enter the Egypt section. This inspires a mounting sermon about Moses, the Israelites, and the house of bondage.

Jonny tries to nix it. Nodding to the nearby mummies on display, he chances a jest. 'The house of *bandage*, more like.'

The jest dies a fast and ignoble death.

'They didn't l*earn*.' Eamon testifies.

'Didn't learn what?'

'They were given their freedom, and what did they do with it?'

Oh dear.

The silly fucker is using this old chestnut to illustrate Jonny's predicament—of his seemingly squandered freedom.

'They certainly learned what freedom meant,' Jonny challenges. 'The freedom to get it wrong. The freedom to waste it. The freedom to learn from their mistakes. Isn't that what God wants? Where does it say we have to get it right first time without getting smitten and smotten and smote and all that?'

'No sooner had Moses delivered them from slavery and gone to the mountain, the people who should have been grateful, instead they made a—'

'Yeah, yeah, a golden calf.'

'A graven image! They were finally free of Egyptian tyranny and they squandered that freedom on crime and the worship of false idols.'

Jonny had been force-fed all this since the cradle and knew it back to front. He loved these stories but drew the line at using them to bolster pointless arguments about how to live in this day and age—especially Jonny's life in this day and age.

'In all fairness,' Jonny replies, diplomatically, 'Moses had gone off the get the basic template of how to act—and took his time about it, it must be said—and didn't exactly have a guidebook, so to speak, until he returned with the Ten Commandments. So, only *then* did they have the instructions of how to properly live and worship. They were yet to read the rules.'

'They had no faith,' Eamon states again. 'They didn't learn!'

Eamon's sermon will not be nixed. As he drones on, Jonny's attention zones out. Somewhere noisy might do the trick, and Jonny knows just the place.

Annoyingly, the trio playing that early evening session at the 2i's coffee bar are playing some meandering folk bollocks. Back in '58, when he first got down here, he'd been too late for Tommy Steele, but just in time for Cliff and the Drifters. He'd seen some great Rock 'n' Roll groups since, and thought this would be just the place to drown out his father's droning sermons. But today it was some blonde bird, all in black, with a couple of bearded teacher types strumming acoustic guitars. What made it worse was they started singing some bordering-on-the-religious songs.

He's got the whole world in his hands?

For fuck's sake.

There was only so much espresso and teacher-music you could take. So, it was time to take off.

He didn't much care for the prospect of spending a night in that bedsit with his father snoring the place to kingdom come, but the earlier they got on with it the earlier Jonny could get him out and on the train home in the morning.

They ascend the narrow staircase out of the tiny underground bar and onto the street. It's dark now. The air is cool. The spicy aroma of exotic foods teases Jonny to distraction. One day, he would sample them all. Soho was always a-buzz, always on, and tonight is no exception. All the mad ones are out, the sharp-suited Jew-boy Jazzers, lost Rockers, Greasers, people off the telly, the down and outs, killers, thugs, the French boys, the bowler-hatted home office suits on the prowl for . . . God only knows what. Just being here and people-watching had passed many an otherwise uneventful night. Jonny discovered wrestlers owned half of the bars and clubs in Soho, including the one they just came out of. And if Nicky Nash's scattershot intel was to be believed, gangsters of 'Rich' Clifford Sherman and Sammy Fortnoy's ilk owned the other half. According to the bespectacled one, the Krays never made a serious play for action around here because of said wrestlers—man mountains who didn't need cudgels and blades: men who would break your back just for the sheer fun of kicking your wheelchair over next time they saw you—and those unhinged twins knew they'd have their hands full with Sherman's firepower. Sherman was one of the first mobsters savvy enough to know that having the Bill in your pocket was the only way forward. The Bill issued their *licenses* to Sherman to keep his "book shops" unmolested. But if said cops didn't cotton on to the fact that every transaction—made as they were in pub toilets and the back seats of Sherman's Bentleys—were being meticulously taken note of, they really weren't paying due and proper attention. That's why the old queen was the king around here: Queen Kong, Nicky called Sherman. Jonny would own a piece of this kingdom one day, but right now, he was happy to be one of its subjects. Soho was the greatest show on earth!

As they wander down Old Compton Street, Jonny decides to have a bit of fun with the old man and lead him through the valley of death ... Tisbury Court.

You get a nose full of their soapy aroma first as they sidle alongside you. In a flurry of leather, lace and trowel-administered makeup, the tarts are on them like Robert Morley on a free lunch. 'Two quid fra quickie, or I'll give yer an 'and job fer ten bob!'

Eamon's head seems to descend into his chest cavity as he quickens his pace to a fast trot to escape the women's attentions. 'Oh, terrible ... terrible ...'

'Not terrible at all,' Jonny corrects him. 'That's the going rate.'

By the time they reach the relative sanctuary of Berwick Street, the old man inhabits a state somewhere between rage and relief.

They share a smouldering silence on the bus that takes them back west. The old man is seemingly struck dumb until they reach Jonny's bedsit. They can hear Stefania's television blaring out and know she's safely glued to its screen.

Once ensconced in Jonny's room, an attempt to lighten Eamon's mood backfires . . . spectacularly.

'Listen, if you wanted take any of those girls up on it, I wouldn't say a word to Mam.'

And that's when violence ensues. Whatever awesome power it was that has contained Eamon's ire for the last hour is punctured by this remark. His flying fist is a haymaker and had it connected, would have sent Jonny to a darkness where all receivers of such blows find themselves in sweet repose. The scuffle that follows and finds his father on the floor is over in half a minute. Jonny backs off, keeping watch for any more surprise attacks. The routine is a familiar one, but no less tiresome for it.

'Want some porridge? I'll put some on if you behave yourself.'

'One of these days . . .'

Jonny gives his father a scant once-over, looking for signs of excess weight or diminished musculature. The man's suit and loose shirt thwart any such promise. He is still in good shape, but on the wrong side of being a serious threat . . . to Jonny, at least.

The moment is fractured when both men hear hurried thuds coming up the stairs and urgent knocking, probably a complaint about the noise. Stefania doesn't wait for the *come in* and enters the room in a hurry. She regards the two men with the same wry eye that Eamon still had on Jonny from the floor. It strikes Jonny as comical, the way she ignores the stranger struggling to his feet and turns her attention to Jonny. 'It's Danny. He's downstairs.'

Before Jonny descends the landing, he already knows what this is about. Jane's kid brother and sister, Connie, are waiting on the doorstep and hurriedly confirm his fears.

Jonny comes back into the room where his father has taken over porridge duties.

Jonny grabs his jacket from the back of the door. 'I gotta go. You can stay here tonight, but tomorrow you be gone.'

Eamon's mouth gapes like a hooked sprat. 'Wha . . . where are you going?!'

Jonny stops and turns to face his father.

Confession time.

'Look, dad, you might as well know now, I'm married and my wife's about to have a baby.'

If it was possible for a man's ghast to be any more flabbered, Eamon manages it. The mouth gapes just that little bit faster. For the second time tonight the man is rendered mute. First, by those Tisbury Court tarts and now this.

'Tell the folks back home to go and fuck themselves.' Then Jonny recants. 'Except Mam. Don't say that to Mam.'

He punches his way into the sleeves of his jacket, glances warily at the bed where his titty mags are hidden and is gone.

How or why Jane is in a hospital on the other side of the river remains a mystery for the time being. It will later become apparent that she was visiting a friend in Balham yesterday when her waters broke. *The South London Hospital for Women*, across the Road from Clapham Common, was the nearest place they could take her. The kids told him that they and their mum had been with her all day on the ward, but she was alone in her own room now.

It shakes him to see her so worn out and pale. She is having a tough time of it according to the nurse—a *tough* beyond Jonny's scope. Attempting to distract her from her pain and distress, he tells her about his dad's surprise visit—and about the day out—but not about the devastating news of Paul Ingram's death and the fight that concluded it.

'That's nice,' she says.

Jonny chuckles sardonically.

The nurse comes back and asks him to step outside while she busies herself around Jane's bed. He paces the hallway, forlorn and helpless. The nurse comes out of the room, gaunt and harried, in a uniform of starched hard white, and beckons him back in.

'You may as well go home, Mr Arnold. The contractions have abated; she's not in established labour so we don't expect much action for a while yet. You should come back in the morning.'

Jonny ignores her and turns to Jane. 'I'll be back in a couple of hours. I'll sleep on one of them benches in the hallway if I have to. '

Jane smiles a feeble acknowledgement and drifts into sleep.

It's nearly nine now. How to kill a few hours? *The Vikings* is showing on a rerun at the Balham Ritz. Jonny has seen it twice already, but it is a fucking great film, so he has no qualms about seeing it again. He gets his ticket from the kiosk and can feel eyes on him. Not from the spotty Herbert that serves him from behind the glass, but from somewhere behind him. Outside, through the entrance doors, a fat man in a grey suit and turtle-neck sweater is stamping out a roll up and catches Jonny returning his gaze. The man, bulldog-solid on short, stubby legs, comes inside and waddles over. Nothing about the man's approach offers a clue as to his intent. Jonny pockets his ticket and braces himself for an attack. First his father and now this. What a fucking day.

The man's hand shoots out to shake. 'Tarzan! I thought it was you! Where ya bin?'

Reflex has Jonny shake the stranger's confident grip, but the face—fiftyish, ruddy-faced, broken nose, balding, looks like Ernest Borgnine—remains a head scratcher.

'Jock Hammer's been trying to reach ya, but no-one knows where to get a hold o' ya.'

Jonny feigns recognition, but the man clocks it.

'Silly cunt, you don't remember me, do ya?' He chuckles an unoffended wheeze. '*Eddie*. Hammerstone's ring crew. I was at the Catford show. Fuck, you held your own, kid. There ain't many who can go that long with that fucking maniac. Everyone expected you to end up next to the Dominator.'

All former recollections of this man will remain forever mysterious, but Jonny will remember him from now on.

'You were there?'

'Oh yeah, great match! Hewitt didn't know what hit him. Those Lancashire Turns were top-notch!'

Again, with the *Lancashire Turns*. Jonny will have to find out what the fuck they are. It seemed he had moves that even *he* didn't know he had.

'All I remember is that he hit me . . . once or twice.'

'Yeah, well, he had to work for it, the prick. Half o' this game's all about being able to take a twatting, and you certainly took one a them. The boys were delighted. Mucho impresario. They wanna use ya. Where you bin?'

'Here and there.'

'Here and there? *Cunt.* Call 'em! They wanna talk to ya.'

The man gestures to the big lobby posters flanking the theatre's entrance. '*He* was a wrestler, y'know, Kirk Douglas—'

'Yeah, I know.'

'—before he became a film star.'

Fourteen other people are in attendance at this nine-twenty showing, including Eddie, who has gone over to sit with a woman in a big fur coat.

The day was action-packed, to say the least. The unpleasant surprise of his dad's visit, the devastating news of Paulie's death, he himself on the brink of fatherhood . . . it was too much to take in. Vikings be his saviour now . . .

Jonny's eyes are on Kirk and Tony Curtis as they get into it, both hoping to get into Janet Leigh. Ernest Borgnine's appearance in the film is a weird coincidence and Jonny can't help riff on the idea that the likeness of the bringer of good tidings—in the shape of ring rat Eddie—is some kind of omen. Yeah, Jonny's eyes are all over *The Vikings*, but his head is swimming with Eddie's revelation—that Hammerstone's were looking for *him*. Despite his bullshit win, he knew he lost that Catford match in no uncertain terms. And they were *impressed*?! His naivety insists this made no sense, but what he does sense is that he is on the precipice of an uncharted logic.

The film ends. The lights come up and the fourteen people exit the cinema and out onto a darkening high road. Ring rat Eddie and his woman are nowhere to be seen.

By the time Jonny gets to the top of Balham Hill, all the streetlights were on. The flower stall outside Clapham Common tube station is closing up. He buys a bunch of daffodils. The yellow flowers seem crestfallen in his hand.

He reaches Jane's ward but cannot find the room.

He turns to see a nurse approaching. Not the same one as before . . . happier . . . jauntier . . .

'Mr Arnold?'

'Yeah, where is she?'

'You are now the father of a beautiful baby girl.'

'She's had it?! They said it . . . *she* . . . wouldn't be here till tomorrow.'

'Mother nature has her own agenda, Mr Arnold. She will do what she must *when* she must.'

This nurse strikes Jonny as overly poetic for this job. He is disinclined to engage her on a similar level. 'Where is she, Mrs Arnold?'

The words feel funny in his mouth. *Mrs Arnold*.

'This way . . .'

The baby's face is a scrunched donut of purple flesh. He tenderly strokes the boneless nub of her nose. He places his palm across her little hot head. Whatever . . . *whoever* Jonny was, shifts. He knows he is forever changed . . . forever off-balance. His self-assigned role as a lone aggressor has been removed. He is now a protector.

Jane lies in a half-sleep, exhausted with creation.

She has made a person.

Heroic.

Godlike.

And yet ... somehow ... grimy.

Godlike and grimy ...

She registers his presence. Without opening her eyes, she croaks, 'Where were you?'

Her voice is barely recognisable, hoarse as it is with the unimaginable exertions of the last couple of hours: hours during which he'd sat watching a film.

'I was here. I came straight away. They told me it—*she*—wouldn't be here till tomorrow.'

His eyes are fixed on the baby's serene face—ugly and beautiful. 'Told me to get lost.'

To Jonny, Jane is somehow reborn. 'I got flowers.'

He places the flowers on his wife's chest like you would a corpse, then quickly puts them on the chair bedside her.

'There was no way I was gonna stay away and miss this.'

'Well, you did.' She smiles a wearied smile. The admonishment is without malice. He is here now.

He gazes again at the baby's face ... her tiny hands. He holds them, studies her purple nails. Already her face begins to take on a natural hue as the oxygen takes hold and ushers her into this life.

'This Italy thing ... I might not have to go now.'

'Oh ...'

'I might have sorted something out.'

He thinks better of raising the subject of what happened to Paulie. The first thing fatherhood was teaching him was that the future was now considered through a vastly different lens. He knew they would remember this moment for the rest of their days and Jonny didn't want to sully it with elements of death to contaminate the memory. There is a time and place for that news and this isn't it.

Jonny reaches into the cot, picks the baby up, holds her gently against his chest and sniffs her dark matted hair.

'She smells of toffee or something. What are we calling her?'

'Ava.'

'Ava? You've already decided?'

Jane succumbs to a deep and sudden sleep.

The sleep of the just . . .

He has no argument, so Ava it will be.

Left alone with the two sleeping females, Jonny shakes the tiny fist of his daughter.

'Hello, little lady, I'm so glad you're here.'

10. KUDOS

Jock Hammer is on the phone when Jonny bounds into the office that late September morning. Boss man shoulders the handset for a second and mouths *be wiv yer in mo* and carries on his gruff negotiations with whoever is on the other end.

Jonny is in no hurry. It's like the more time he is in here—in this Brixton head-quarters—the more he is part of it. He wanders around looking at the pulpy posters of antiquity and the framed photos of Jock and Gil posing with Prince Phillip; with Peter Ustinov and some posh looking bird that Jonny doesn't recognise . . . he can already see the day when his own posters are on this wall.

Speaking of which, some kid comes in holding out a still wet poster, fresh off Hammerstone's basement printing presses. Jock nods a quick approval. The kid disappears as quick as he came.

Jock puts the phone down and cuts straight to it. 'Alright Jonny. Sit down. You did good in Catford. Not many can tangle with Kelly Hewitt and walk properly afterwards.'

Jonny spins a chair and sits. 'I'll have him next time.'

'You might have to wait a while for that. We've had to take him off the cards for a while. He's looking at criminal proceedings for that Croydon mess. You know Farrago died, right?'

'The Dominator's dead?'

'Never came out of the coma. His missus is chasing Hewitt for manslaughter, so it wouldn't be proper to have him on until the whole thing gets settled.'

Jock studies Jonny to see if this news shakes him any. Jonny meets Jock's appraisal with as blank a countenance as he can muster, but inwardly, this was a fucking shocker. He survived a match with a certified killer!

Jonny's response, or lack thereof, seems to satisfy the boss man. 'A little dickie bird tells me you've just done a bit of time.'

'I chinned a copper. Got me three weeks in the Scrubs.'

'Zat right?'

'Yeah, it is.'

Jock considers this and continues. 'So, when you're not chinnin' coppers, whatcha y'doin' for work?'

'You tell me.'

'No, I mean daytime.'

'Nothing. Zero. Zilch,' Jonny lies. Desperation might work for him. Besides, his current status as a road digger might tarnish whatever star quality he might convey.

'You got a kid, ain't ya?'

'Have now.'

'So, how are you surviving?'

'*This*. Wrestling. If and when. The independents: DeMarto's, Oscars . . . Jim Osprey's lot . . .'

'Just wrestling?'

Jonny nearly mentions the Italian adventure—if only to emphasise said star quality, but decides to play the meagre option card. 'What else? It's what I was born for.'

'This ain't America, son. There's no such thing as a *professional* wrestler. Those boys out there? — they're all lorry drivers and bouncers in the cold light. This is a sideline. Most of them are only in it to impress their birds at the weekend.'

This isn't what Jonny's come to hear. 'What do you want to see me about, Jock?'

Jock slides a sheet of notepaper across the desk towards him. 'Salisbury, Nottingham, Leeds and Manchester. I take it I'm not being too previous in thinking you're available?'

Jonny's eyes devour the paper like an ancient tract. 'No, you ain't. So, am I signed?'

Jock holds up a halt-hand. 'Wait for the bugle, duchess. We'll do a few round 'ere first and see how you go. You drive?'

'Not yet. But I can get there. Don't worry about that.'

'We got our own transport. But it leaves from here.'

'Really? Great. Even better.'

Jock reclines in his chair and considers Jonny with that practised eye. 'The game's really taking off right now and a lot more birds are coming to the matches. I s'pose for them it's like us going to see a stripper. They wanna see dolly fellas and . . . well . . . you fit that criterion.' Jock re-appraises the contained explosion of hunger and ambition before him. 'You know what you could do with, though? A gimmick.'

'A gimmick?'

'Something that looks good on the posters—give 'em something to remember you by. Look at the Dominator—God rest him, and Dr Dread, The Egyptian and Bobi. They all got gimmicks. Once seen, never forgotten.'

'I ain't wearing no mask. I was made to be seen. And Bobi? what's his gimmick?' Jonny gestures to the big poster of the man on the wall behind Jock. 'Them leopard-skin trunks?'

'Jonny, the man's black. He was born a gimmick.'

Wherever Nicky Nash is, he dominates proceedings, as he does now on this bright morning, holding court in Vern's café. Him and some of the boys crowd around a small table by the window. The *letch window*, they call it—a prime spot from which passing females can be ogled and assessed. Anyone *not* at the letch table is devouring one of Vern's thrombosis specials. There is a lull in the parade on Brixton High Road—a few old ladies, harried males, but no assessable females in view.

Dazzler Damien Logan picks up the slack and continues his account of a recent conquest. 'So, I showed her my one-eyed trouser snake, and she said, *blimey, will it hurt?* So, *I* said, well, it's never killed anyone, but it's made a few people dizzy.'

The court is in an uproar, but Nicky never really laughs properly. Never from the gut. He guffaws quietly behind his cigarette.

'That's one of mine!' Evan protests.

Damien continues, 'So, she sez, *if it's that big we shouldn't do it then.* So, I sez, why not? And she sez, *I've got a bad heart.* So, I sez, well, lay on your side and I'll miss it!'

Big laughs all round.

This is the state of play that Jonny chances upon as he enters—King Nick attended to by his jesters. Coffee machine steam and cigarette smoke render the scene opaque.

Jonny nods. It's a general nod, meant for anyone who sees it. He's surprised to see Kelly Hewitt at a far table, eating alone—a long way from his Yorkshire pig farm and a long way from humanity. He'd have thought that he'd been arrested or something. The way Hewitt looks at Jonny, anyone would think he'd never seen him before.

Evan spots Jonny also as he squeezes his way between tables and chairs towards the counter and shouts across the room, 'Seen the film, read the book, now *meet* Tarzan!'

The group look over at Jonny. The laughter ramps. Mirth maintained.

Damien thumbs in Jonny's direction and says, 'He's another one that'll fuck anything that moves.'

'Yeah, and if it don't move—' Evan swoops in, beautifully, '—he'll fuck it till it does!'

Jonny brings over his glass of milk and pulls up a chair. 'Oh, you funny cunts.'

Finally, over the road, three young women—lookers—cross and pass the café, oblivious to the men behind the glass. Maybe the reflection of the mid-morning sun obliterates their presence. Maybe years of male judgment have been eradicated by tiresome familiarity.

Evan clocks them. 'Hang on! Hang on! Look at these.'

Everyone *looks at these*.

In an Irish accent, Damien chirps, 'Brings a lump to your trousers, so it does.'

Nicky doesn't so much as *watch* as absorb. 'They've got stockings and garter belts on as well,' he observes sagely.

Evan says, 'From *here* you can tell that?'

'Birds walk different in sozzies. They got a swagger you don't see when they're in slacks.'

The boys consider this pearl. Evan crushes it. 'Yeah, well, you can always tell whether a bird's wearing knickers or not.'

In unison, at least three of the boys ask, 'Yeah, how?'

'Dandruff on the toenails.'

Everyone laughs big. Oh yeah, the comedy never stops. It's as if something unbearable is primed and loaded to pounce on them if it did.

Evan turns to Jonny. 'So, what did Gil have for ya?'

The boys are noisy. Jonny has to shout. 'What?!'

'I heard Gil l wanted to see you!'

'No. Jock. Gil's a cunt. I'm on a few cards for next month.'

'What happened to Italy? Thought you were going off to be a film star.'

'You heard about that?'

'Yeah.'

'Nah. I'm taking my cue from Napoleon. "When you set out to take Vienna, take Vienna!"'

'Bone-Apart said that?'

'No, not that Belgian twat. The *actual* Napoleon.'

'Didn't know you knew him. So, what they give ya?'

'Nottingham, Manchester, Salisbury and another one.'

'Leeds?'

'Yeah.'

'Same as me. I'll see ya on the road then, boy! How're you gettin' there?'

'Jock says they've got buses or something.'

'Ah no! Not them fucking converted ambulances! They break down every other show. Don't bother with them. If they break down and you don't make the match, they won't pay ya. Get a car.'

'I need to earn first. Catch-22 and all that.'

'If you're in the market for a motor, talk to Nick, e's got a cab firm. 'E's got loads o' cars.' Evan puts on his American advert voice. *'Would you buy a used car from this man?'*

Damien says, 'Yeah, I'd buy a car, but I'd be fucked if I'd buy a plane off him.'

They all laugh, except Nicky, who says, 'What the fuck you on about?'

Damien points at the bespectacled one. 'It's *him* though, 'innit?'

Everyone eyes the man in the thick horn-rims.

Nicky eyes the joker. In fact, *four-eyes* the joker. 'It's who?'

'Buddy Holly.'

Laughter.

Nicky doesn't entertain piss takers. 'Fuck off.'

Hewitt-the-killer growls from over in his corner. 'Yeah, Buddy Holly with acne!'

Laughter.

For an instant Nicky's feeble eyes fix Kelly Hewitt with permafrost—like he's working out where to put him on some list—then snaps out of it and addresses his immediate audience. 'I don't think you fully appreciate what an insult that is. I saw his show a few years ago. What a load of bollocks.'

Jonny is interested. 'Saw who? Buddy Holly? Where?'

'The Troc, if my memory fails me correctly.'

'Elephant and Castle?'

Damien says, 'I thought you hated all that Yank crap, Nick.'

'I do. Anyway, he weren't a Yank, he was a fucking redneck.'

'Ain't he dead?' Evan enquires.

Kelly growls. 'Go on, trigger.'

Damien, never slow to deliver, says, 'I fuckin' hope so—they buried him!'

Laughter.

Jonny, undeterred, demands information. 'How come you saw him then?'

'It wasn't *him* I went to see,' Nicky answers. 'I was knocking off one of the Tanner Sisters at the time. They were on the same bill.'

'Seriously? What was he like?'

'I told ya, *fuckin' useless*. You hear all them records, *Raining In My Heart* or whatever, but it was nothing like that. It was twenty minutes of him jumping up and down shouting Little Richard tunes. And that fucking thing he was using for a guitar! What a row. I mean, you see guitars like that all the time now, but then, it was like, *what the fuck is that*? Still got the 'eadache.'

'I take it you don't like Little Richard either?'

'*Oh yeah* . . . I'm a *big* Little fan.'

Laughter.

'Did you speak to him?'

'Speak to who? Little Richard?'

'*To Buddy Holly, Mr Memory*!'

'To be honest, I was more interested in getting the Tanner Sisters to go 'twos up—', Nicky laughs that chokey laugh. '—but they weren't having none of it.'

'I've known you all this time. You never said nothing about seeing Buddy Holly.'

'Well, it weren't exactly a high point in my life, know what I mean?' The subject is a bore. Nicky changes it. 'Did you say you was after a motor?'

'Not yet. I don't have a license for a start.'

'Fuck that, neither do I. Never got around to it. You can drive though?'

'How hard can it be?'

'You got a job in Manchester?'
'Yeah.'
Nicky stands up and whips out his car keys. 'C'mon, I might be able to sort you out.'

On the gravel-strewn forecourt of the Hammerstone building, between two of their converted painted blue ambulances, sits a huge glossy black slab of American automation.

Jonny spots it a mile off. Got to be Nicky's. 'Galaxie. Nice.'

'Galaxie 500XL,' Nicky corrects. 'Nicer.'

Nicky vaults over the low wall that separates the forecourt from the pavement and gets in. Jonny waits for Nicky to unlock the passenger door.

Nicky says, 'It's open.'

The car lurches out on to the high road.

Jonny runs his hand over the lux dash. 'Where do you even get these things?'

'I got connections. Import 'em in from a dealership in California.'

Using his elbows to steer, Nicky sparks up a cigarette and offers the pack.

'You know I don't.'

'Nicky flings the pack onto the dash. 'I'm always needing bits and pieces dropped off here and there. If you're gonna be going up and down the country, you might be interested in making some deliveries for me. Work it into your curriculum as it were.'

'Deliveries of what?'

'Blueys. Dirty films.'

A two-tone Hillman cuts in front of Nicky.

Nicky honks. 'Oi, you fuckin' prat!'

A mutual sequence of two-finger salutes and wanker signals ensues.

'Fuckin' prat . . .' Nicky makes a mental note of the registration for future reference.

'I got a little photographic place in Streatham,' Nicky continues. 'I'll go into more detail when we get there. I just gotta pop in and say hello to a mate first.'

At traffic lights, Nicky spots two nuns waiting to cross on Railton Road. 'I don't know what it is, but whenever I see a nun, I'm filled with this overwhelming desire to expose myself.'

'Please don't.'

Nicky winds the window down, points at his crutch and shouts, 'Come and confirm this, Bernadette!'

Opposite Brixton Prison, Nicky takes a sudden left and pulls up in Elm Park.

He gets out.

Somewhere up the way, the walking bass-line of *We Are Rolling* by Stranger Cole throbs from an open window.

Jonny says, 'Shall I wait here or—?

'No. Come with. You can meet Tony.'

Jonny follows Nicky up a short garden path of cracked patterned tiles, to a solid red brick terraced house. The door and bay windows are obscured by a high hedge.

Apart from the booming music up the way, the area exudes cosy suburbia.

Nicky taps the knocker and rings the bell.

Nothing.

He taps harder and rings again.

He listens for movement inside.

Through the frosted glass in the door, they see someone approaching.

Nicky stands back waiting for it to open. It doesn't.

Behind the door, a voice. 'Who is it?'

'It's me: Nicky.'

The door opens slightly, but the chain is still on. Eyes appear at the gap. The voice says, 'Hello Nick. How's it going?'

'Let us in, Tone.'

There is fumbling. A voice, jocular, nervous, says, 'Wwwwhat's the password, Nick?'

'Klaatu barada nikto. Just open the fuckin' door.'

The chain rattles loose and Nicky shoulders his way inside. Jonny follows.

Jonny has already clocked the scent of leather and sandalwood incense before they reach the lounge that Tony leads them to. In the centre of the room is a low coffee table made from a slice of a three-foot-wide tree encased in thick varnish. The sofa is covered with genuine zebra skins. There are African drums, masks and wooden carvings everywhere. Dominating an entire wall is a beautifully detailed but gaudy rug, depicting two tigers on a mountain. The whole thing is made from real skins and furs and would not be out of place in a Rhodesian knocking shop.

Nicky sits on the hide-covered sofa and sparks up. Tony clocks Jonny's physique and shuffles uneasily with his back to the window.

Jonny is impressed with everything in the room: the tigers-on-a-mountain rug in particular. 'Woah! Where d'ya buy this?'

Tony keeps a wary eye on Nicky as he answers. 'It weren't so much bought, as acquired.'

Nicky draws tightly on his cigarette and gets to it. 'Wanda about?'

'She's in town.'

Nicky considers this and turns to Jonny. 'Could you do us a favour, Jonny, and put the kettle on? I've just got to sort something out with Tony.'

Jonny is not comfortable with the concept of being sent to make tea, especially in a stranger's house, but Jonny reads the room. There's more to this than a friendly visit. 'Where's the kitchen?'

Nicky knows and tells him. 'Down the hall on the right. Cheers, Jonny.'

An acrid chemical odour assails his nostrils before he gets there, and Jonny is shocked to find a pile of orange rubber dildos on the kitchen table. Next to the sink is a row of five plaster moulds filled with steaming orange molten rubber.

Out in the lounge, Nicky outlines the situation. 'What're your maths like, Tone?'

'Uh?'

'Your maths, Tony, your fuckin' *maths*.'

'Uh?'

'Don't fuck me about.' In a heavy onyx ashtray, Nicky prematurely stubs out his cigarette. 'The numbers on your pickups are seriously iffy.'

'Well, they *shouldn't* be.'

'You're tellin' *me* they shouldn't be! But they are and it's adding up like this: the first delivery was down a ton. The second delivery was also—correct me if I'm wrong—a ton short. Now,' Nicky sighs big, 'somewhere between retail and *you*, there's a gaping discrepancy. Surely you must appreciate that such conduct is detrimental to our industry, Tone. Yes? Now, on a personal level, I don't give a flying fuck. It's not my cash. I'm merely here in a middleman capacity. But the hero's dilemma—the hero being me—is this: does one go back to Eric and Peter with good tidings of a square account? Or does one deliver unto Eric and Peter your fucking eyes in a jar?'

Jonny walks into the room with a full tray, oblivious to the heat. 'Love the ornaments.'

Without taking his bespectacled eyes off Tony, Nicky asks, 'What's that?'

Jonny addresses Tony. 'Those things you've got in the kitchen.'

'What you got in the kitchen, Tone?'

'I'm doing some of those dicks for Vic.'

'Vic the prick?'

'Dicks for Vic.'

Nicky's gotta see this, so does.

Left alone, Jonny and Tony exchange glances. Jonny's of mild confusion: Tony's of creeping apprehension. The man is tanned, good looking—in a Robert Wagner sort of way—and wearing the kind of embroidered silk robe more suited to Jonny's landlady.

Nicky comes back into the room with a paper carrier bag full of dildos and dumps them on the table. 'Right! Money!'

'I don't know what the fuck you're on about.'

'*Tony*, you made a pickup in Dean Street this morning, and by the time it arrived in Belgravia, there was yet another hundred quid missing. I didn't want to change the subject violently, but you're making me change the subject violently.'

'Nick, for fuck's sake, cool it—'

Something comes over Nicky: as if his public personality has been slid away like a stage set, revealing a much darker scene. 'Right. You and Henry are gonna have to sort this out between the two of you.'

'*Henry*? Who the fuck is Henry?'

Nicky pulls out a flick-knife—standard hoodlum issue—from somewhere behind his back and switches the blade.

For Jonny, the penny descends.

Nicky goes into a routine that Jonny suspects is not off the cuff.

Nicky gives it the big theatrical sigh and holds up the knife. 'Tony, this is Henry. Henry—'

Nicky lunges forward in a fencing-like attack, lightning speed, then skips neatly away from the bloody carnage that is a screaming Tony as he slides down the wall, nursing a punctured cheek.

'—meet Tony.'

Nicky and Jonny load the rolled-up tigers-on-a-mountain wall carpet into the boot of the car. Nicky throws the bag of rubber dicks onto the back seat.

Jonny is shaken, but holds it down. 'Bit strong, weren't it?'

Nicky's mind is already on his next move. 'What was?'

'The shiv. *Henry*.'

Nicky walks around the car, pulls a bundle of tenners from an inside pocket, peels a couple off and hands them over. 'They always cough up once they've clocked your chassis.'

'Yeah?' Jonny pockets the notes. 'Like a blade in the face had nothing to do with it.'

'Believe me, I know how to gauge these situations. Taking drastic measures means we haven't got to stand around all day talking about the Cooper/Clay fight, or how Tottenham did last Wednesday.'

Back on the highroad, on that A23 going south, Nicky sparks another fag and again offers one to Jonny. Jonny says 'No,' and waves it off.

'Don't you know that the road of excess leads to the palace of wisdom?'

'No, it leads to the shithouse of lung cancer.'

'Do you have a vice, Jon?'

'Yeah, trying to live forever, or die tryin'.'

'You shouldn't measure the quality of a life by its length. Live now. Die later. That's one of my many mottos.'

'Yeah, well . . . I'm planning on outstaying my welcome and I don't fancy spending the last twenty years of it in a pram.'

'I heard you went away.'

Jonny side-longs him. Those dickie birds get around, don't they?

'I chinned a copper.'

'Yeah? That's a relief.'

'How's that a relief?'

'They reckon you got caught giving someone a nosh in an alley.'

'Yeah? Well, point me in the direction of who *reckoned* that and I'll un-reckon 'em quick-fast. Who said that?'

'No one specific. That seems to be the general—'

'If any cunt wants to say that to my face, I'll kick their fucking face off! Who said it?!'

'Relax! *Fuck*! No-one knows *anything*. The whole lot of 'em are full of shit—vague at best. Why'd you think they call this place the smoke?' Nicky recalibrates, inhales and blows. 'This wrestling lark—are you a blue eye or a heel?'

Nicky's penchant for pulling sudden tangents in a conversation is an annoyance. Jonny figures it's his way of keeping people off balance. Or maybe it's just some silly game he plays with himself. But they're on Jonny's subject now, so he goes with it.

'Fuck knows. I'm strictly preliminary material for the time being.'

'You know what you need? A gimmick.'

'Yeah, that has been mentioned.'

'Whatever you do, you got to be a heel though. You look too much like a blue eye. You got to be a villain. Everyone loves a good villain.'

Again, with the gimmick advice . . . Clearly, being a superb wrestler is a mere formality. The subject is tiresome. Jonny pulls a tangent of his own.

'That Cooper/Clay fight . . . what d'ya make of it?'

Nicky sucks the life out of his fag—'There's no way Cooper put 'im down.'—and flings the butt out of the window. 'Clay's a showman. He threw us a fucking bone.'

A man and a woman are fucking on the bonnet of a Humber Hawk. Another couple are similarly engaged in the back seat. The women are topless, with their skirts up around their waists. The men keep their shirts on with their trousers around their ankles. The scene has been staged in a forest on a sunny day. The scratchy 8mm film cuts monotonously from one couple to the other, until the reel flicks off its spool.

Nicky switches the light on.

The studio is stacked, floor to ceiling, with boxes of films and shelved camera equipment. The walls, festooned with drying 8 x 10s clipped to washing lines across the room.

Jonny has never seen anything like it: *actual* film of people going *at it*.

Moving colour film of *the thing*!

Jonny's magazines, at best, were a few tit shots and the pubic region air-brushed out. This room is a wanker's paradise. Jonny shines nonchalant. His dick, however, is not a hypocrite. He shifts casually to conceal the effect.

'Where do you find the girls for these things?'

'You kidding? Half the time they come looking for *me*. You'd be amazed what a girl will do after a few Babychams.'

Immediately, a movie camera appears at the top of Jonny's shopping list as soon as the money starts rolling in.

'But see, that's the beauty of our operation,' Nicky continues. 'While everybody else in this game are importing their stuff from abroad, and half the time having it seized at customs, all our stuff is home grown. In fact, we're shipping our stuff out to *them*!'

Jonny picks up some boxes of films from the table beside him and reads from the gaudy artwork.

'Made in Hamburg . . . Made in Copenhagen . . . Made in Burbank, Cal . . . *Burbank, Cal*? Where's that?'

'California. But we actually print 'em here, for fuck's sake. I can say they were made on the fucking *moon* if I want to. Keeps the straighter elements of the Flyin' Squad looking the wrong way. I shoot most of 'em here in the studio. The one you've just seen was done in Epping Forest. The bird in the black wig, that's my wife, incidentally.'

'Your wife?! That weren't you fucking her, though.'

'Nah. That was Taffy. Ex wrestler from your neck of the woods, funnily enough. Tough Taffy Jones, they called him. Know him?'

'Never heard of him.'

'One of the old school. Fucked his legs in a match in Ilfracombe a couple of years ago. Can't wrestle no more, but he's hung like a Peruvian pit pony. So, he's got all the time in the world and all the talent.'

'And you let him fuck your wife? And who's filming it? You?'

'Naturally. She don't do nothing without my say so. She knows what'll fuckin' happen if she did. No, this is business. She's dick mad and I indulge her. But anyway . . . *this* is the centre of operations. Forget the cab firm, forget the camera shop upstairs. All of *that*, fronts for *this*. I'll cut to the chase. Due to the illicit nature of this enterprise, one of the main headaches is distribution. A few of the boys at Hammerstone's—a select few, mind—are making serious moolah carting these things about. Now, the reason you're not getting the time-of-day Jonny, is cos you ain't mobile. Gils's reluctance to have you on board comes from a place of mobility. All the boys who rely on those fucking ambulances are third graders. You wanna be first-grade? You gotta be self-sufficient and *that* means having your own wheels. Jock knows you're keen—that you're a grafter, and once he knows you can get to the shows under your own steam, he'll be putting you on all over the place, and there's *my* incentive.' Nicky let Jonny absorb. 'I tell ya, with the money you could be earning from the game on top of what you'll be making out of doing me a favour, *along* with the loan of the car of course, financial embarrassment will be a thing of the past. Now I know you have a question Jonny and I know what it is, but go on, ask it anyway.'

'The Gestapo. The law. I don't need any more porridge.'

Nicky holds up a *let me stop you right there*, hand. 'Right, here's the story. You get a tug. You get pulled over. They look in the boot. They find a sports bag full of fuck films. *"Are you the owner of this vehicle, sir?" "Fuck - no. This car belongs to a Mr Nicholas Nash Esq who's lending it to me. The car and its contents*, you *Einsatzgruppen fucking twat, are his."* That's right, point 'em to *me*. Then if—and I emphasise the *if*—they come to me, I say *"I own a cab firm. People are always leaving stuff in my cars."* End of story. And worst-case scenario? Some oily little rookie cunt tryin' to make a splash? — there's always Eric and Pete that can step in if the temper dictates. Their licences are always present and correct, so they got half of Scotland Yard in their jockstraps.'

'Eric and Pete?'

'Eric Overman and Peter Devlin. Chaps. Faces. You'll meet them at some juncture. While the Krays and the Richardson's firms are making all the headlines and attracting all the attention, it's Eric and Peter who urinate from a lofty and untouchable height on the lot of 'em. Two steps away from the government, those fuckers. I'm telling you, the only thing you need to worry about, if you *do* get a tug, is not having a driving licence. I only got pulled once. Told 'em it was in the post.'

'Well, if I had the car, I'd take the test.'

'Whatever. That's down to you.'

It's late that same afternoon when the Galaxie 500XL slaloms around the rubble and broken glass scattered on West Row. Nicky pulls up outside Octavia House—Jane's place—that dirty brown brick five storey walk-up in Kensington: untamed Kensington. Not Princess Margret on the prowl for cock and cocaine Kensington.

No.

This is darkie-bashing, queer killing Kensington.

The *other* side of Kensington.

Jane and her mother, Carol, are leaning over the 3rd floor balcony smoking and chatting. On seeing Jonny get out of the unfamiliar car, Jane quickly stubs out her cigarette.

Carol tuts. 'Fuck 'im.'

Nicky pops the boot and drags out Porno Tony's rolled-up tigers-on-a-mountain wall carpet. 'Here.'

'Don't you want it?'

'Don't take the piss. I only *look* like a pimp.'

Jonny scans the street nervously. He looks up and sees Jane and his mother-in-law looking down at him with the potentially 'hot' carpet.

Jane shouts down at him. 'Where you bin?'

Jonny shouts back. 'On safari!'

Nicky squints up and locates the source of the voice. 'Who's that, the missus?'

'Yeah.'

'Nice.'

'Fuck off, you.'

'What?!'

'Just fuck off.'

Jonny lets the carpet slide to his feet and rubs the excess fur from his T-shirt. The boys shake hands.

Nicky is about to get back in the car and shouts to Jonny across the roof. 'Give it some thought and get back to me. I'm telling ya, your bank account won't know what's hit it.'

'What bank account?'

'Well, if you don't call, I'll know it's you.'

Nicky jumps into the car; winds down the window and revs up loud. He reaches over into the back seat and rummages through the carrier bag. The car pulls away, and he throws one of Tony's dildos over the roof at Jonny. 'Here, catch!'

On reflex, Jonny snatches the object out of the air before realising what it is.

Nicky drives off laughing.

Jane and her mother look down at Jonny standing in the street holding the big orange dick.

11. TAKE OFF

They started him local by way of a few warm-ups: Caledonian Baths, Watford Town Hall, and a return to Catford's Lewisham Concert Hall . . . then the world opened up.

Jonny caught buses and trains (and sometimes walked) to the London venues, but further afield, it would have to be the company transport: the converted ambulances. They were freezing, but Jonny didn't care. It was happening. *He* was happening.

As it turned out, Jonny only ever had to use them three times. By the time the out-of-town shows came around, Nicky had given him the use of a near-new white Ford Consul Cortina. Showed him how to start the ignition, change the gears and accompanied him on little drives around his cab place in Norbury. Road signs and traffic lights were easy enough to understand, but finding the biting point on the fucking thing remained a dark art. Once he got moving, he was fine. But those first few days were a series of hard stops and stalls. Within a week, he got the hang of it and he was away.

The M and A roads are a blur. Never really gets to see the towns and cities waiting at the end of them. This late in the year, his arrivals coincide with a gathering darkness, rendering the terrain an encephalograph of jagged silhouettes, sprinkled with twinkling lights. The A–Z Street Atlas becomes his new bible.

His matches are preliminary and although, being as this is the build-up stage, he is fixed to win; he has no doubts about where this is all going. Once the world gets a load of Kid "Tarzan" Jonathan, they will lose their shit!

For the most part, people are still coming in to find their seats by the time his matches conclude. But it was real now.

He is real now.

A real wrestler.

Stepping out of that dressing room into a crowded hall of expectant fans is even more exhilarating than Jonny had ever imagined.

Those amateur matches he'd been doing for the last three years were, for the most part, hosted in community centres and back rooms of hotels, but now it's proper halls . . .

Thursday 3rd Oct. Salisbury City Hall

KID "TARZAN" JONATHAN
vs.
BIG BILLY KING

His first out-of-town match is with Big Billy King. Big Billy is one of the old *'lorry driver's trying to impress their birds'* school. Jonny is unsure where Billy's bird is in the crowd, but he does his utmost to make her un-impressed, and did a pretty good job of it, Jonny felt.

Gil Stone is also unimpressed. He stops Jonny before he leaves for Nottingham. *'Jonny, people want to see a whole match. If you knacker your opponent before the end, they're gonna go home feeling short changed. Give 'em their money's worth. Fuckin' reel it in!'*

Friday 4th Oct. Nottingham Ice Rink

KID "TARZAN" JONATHAN
vs.
"HURRICANE" ROY HARRIS

Okay . . . *reel it in.*

With his next match, he didn't really need to.

The Hurricane is a different proposition altogether. The man is old, but far from out to pasture. Jonny knows he has his hands full from the first round, and if not for a sloppy drop-kick where Jonny side-steps the man and lets him hit his own corner-post knackers-first; the man might have fucked him royally. The Hurricane basically blows himself out and Jonny knows the man won't make the count.

Saturday 5th Oct. Leeds Town Hall

KID "TARZAN" JONATHAN
vs.
CHRIS "CRASH" BANTON

Wrestling with Chris Banton is like trying to ride a tricycle backwards down the stairs. Everything about the man is awkward, and he isn't selling shit. As decreed, Jonny wins, but it's a rubbish win. Jonny vowed to himself that his victories will be spectacular. This was not one of those victories. But Jonny learns on that night that it takes two to be spectacular.

Reel it in.

Make your opponent look good before demolishing him. Then, you'll look even better.

Sunday 6th Oct. Bellevue Arena, Manchester

KID "TARZAN" JONATHAN
vs.
THE BLUE COBRA

The Blue Cobra is a masked mystery from Norwich. He sells beautifully, moves like his namesake and, in his blue satin cowl and cape, looks the business. Tarzan fighting a cobra: It don't get more dramatic than that!

This is the first match where Jonny, in synch with a worthy opponent, really feels that he gives a great show and earns his £4. The roar of that crowd: it's like the future screaming at him.

As for Nicky's 'blueys', Jonny would get a call at the venue to let him know that so and so would be coming and to meet them a local pub or car park. For the most part, the collectors looked as you'd expect. Seedy, dirty mac types in flat caps, smoking roll ups. It was a quick *hello*, hand over the bag, *thank you very much,* and tell Nicky hello.

Clearly, the financial end took place in the distant background. Whether or not this was because Nicky felt that Jonny couldn't be trusted was of no concern at all to Jonny. He got a score up front for each of these drop-offs, and that's all that mattered.

He'd done one in Leeds and one in Manchester. No fuss. No drama. Sweet. A clean, dirty forty quid.

Doncaster, on the other hand, was another story...

Monday 7th Oct. Corn Exchange, Doncaster

KID "TARZAN" JONATHAN
vs.
NOEL POLEON "BONE-APART"

Jonny just got the call. Nicky tells him, *'Derek'll be in the foyer at eight-thirty.'*

This gives him ten minutes. Still perspiring from his match with Bone-Apart, he peeks through the gap in the exit door into the packed hall. Evan is on with the mysterious masked warrior, The Great Mondo.

The Heavenly one is a good technical wrestler—one of the best—and a blue eye, by name, nature and profession.

The masked one is all heel, hell and high drama: shoulders as wide as a bus holding his arms on. At the entrance to the hall, The Great Mondo stops and regards the ocean of fight fans before him, then takes slow, measured steps toward the ring. Once there, he performs his rituals, flexing and warming up before finally removing his long red satin robe.

Reg the ref ushers both fighters into a huddle, gives them the lowdown and gives the signal for the go ahead.

Evan is a solid, *straight down the line* kind of a fighter. None of the guys struck Jonny as tag-team material and Jonny does not consider himself a team player by any stretch. But if he ever had to choose one, Evan "Heaven" Leigh would be it.

The Great Mondo, at six-three, and 20 stone and 4lbs, prowls around the ring with a deceptive lumber. His lightning attacks and even faster defence katas are a dangerous surprise.

The crowd roars their approval as The Great Mondo breaks Evan's Half Nelson all to hell and crotch-lifts him into a body-slam.

Evan lies prone and demolished as the masked man circles, appraising the damage.

The crowd goes wild. The hardboard floor rumbles accordingly.

This is not the way it's supposed to go.

Hurt and bewildered is Evan.

More and more, the crowds seem to favour the bad guys these days. Maybe it's something about the times. The darkening days: the ever-increasing uncertainty of a world spinning off its axis.

Whatever the case, you can see in Evan's baby-blues, even from way across the hall, that he is not happy.

Jonny feels his pain, but it's time to go.

A track-suited Jonny trots into the foyer where the old biddy behind the box office counts the takings into a cash box. Jonny stops and stares at the money.

Without looking up, she asks, 'Can I help?'

'Has anyone called Derek been here asking for me?'

'Sorry, love, just punters.'

'Well, if he turns up, send 'em up to the dressing room or get someone to get me.'

'Well, I'm knocking off soon, but—*Dennis*, is it?'

Jonny walks back across the foyer and shouts back. 'Derek!'

She calls after him. 'Oh, *love*. Who are you?'

He walks over to a wall plastered with an array of identical posters and points to his name near the bottom.

She can't see it from across the foyer. She squints. 'Kip, is it?'

'That's *Kid*. Kid "Tarzan" Jonathan.'

'Bit old to be a kid, ain't ya?'

This sends him off muttering. 'Smart arse.'

The smoky dressing room is busy with fight writers, managers, promoters, hangers-on and the wrestlers themselves.

But no birds!

Unwritten rule.

Save it for the car park or the alleyway. Or a backroom if you can find one.

Jonny's opponent, Noel Poleon 'Bone-Apart', is in the far corner posing for a photographer.

Ring rat Eddie: *Borgnine*, Jonny calls him since that game-changing *Vikings*/Ava birth night in Balham, enters the room with a paper carrier bag. 'Ladies! Ryan's broken down on the A1. He 'ain't gonna make it. Who's gonna be the Dominator tonight?'

Ken the Vampyre is quick to respond. It means another envelope. 'Here.'

Eddie throws the bag at him.

The Vampyre opens and sniffs the dead man's costume. 'I hope this has been washed.'

A final roar from beyond the room signifies the conclusion of Evan's battle with The Great Mondo.

Jonny bounds into the room and zeroes in on his opponent, Noel Poleon, being photographed. The outlandish thing about Noel Poleon 'Bone-Apart' is that he is almost French. *Belgian*, no less. The other shocker: his name really *is* Noel Poleon.

Jonny removes his tracksuit top, flexes up and goes over there. 'What magazine you from?'

The photographer gives Jonny the once over—*dolly fella*—and takes a couple of snaps.

Just as Jonny perfects a pose in which his triceps look particularly incredible, the photographer decides he's got what he wanted and goes back to snapping the 'Frenchman'.

Jonny is quietly furious, but holds it down.

Noel makes the introductions. "E's from *Wrestle Magazine*.'

Jonny puts it to *Mr Wrestle Magazine*, 'Did you get any of my bout?'

'Sorry, son, I don't think so. Which one were you?'

'I was on with *him*. Frenchy.'

'Oh yeah. You're a good little fighter. I'll tell you what you need though.'

'A gimmick?'

'No, some decent publicity photos. Here's my card. I'll give you a good rate.' *Mr Wrestle Magazine* reconsiders. 'Actually, you're right. Get a gimmick.'

'What—', Jonny sneers and gestures dismissively to the Frenchman's head, '—like that tricorn hat?'

'A little bullshit goes a long way in this game, love.'

Jonny pockets the card and walks off muttering, then turns back to the Frenchman. 'Has anyone called Derek been asking for me?'

'Derek? Non.'

Evan storms into the dressing room, ranting. 'What is it with these fuckin' heels, all of a sudden? *I'm* the blue eye, right? I win the fucker and these cunts are giving *me* stick!'

The Frenchman, always in character, channels his inner existentialist. 'The eternal struggle between good and evil is not what was, non?'

Evan channels his inner cunt. 'Piss off, frog!'

Jonny has his own theories. 'You know why? Crumpet-wise, it's a fuckin' drought. There's hardly any birds in tonight.'

Evan, still a-sweat, towel flung over his naked shoulder, fishes a packet of fags from out of his bag. 'I tell you, next match, I'm gonna get that freak's mask off and fuck his gimmick right up.' He sparks up and sucks, furiously.

'No, you won't be doing that!' Eddie shouts across the room.

Mr Wrestle Magazine detects a scoop. 'C'mon, give us an exclusive. Who is he really?'

Evan exhales big, through pursed lips. 'Fuck knows. Apparently, he just turned up at a match in Barnsley, already in his gear, and Gil hired him on the spot.'

This is a hard pill to swallow for Jonny, having nearly got killed by Hewitt for *his* shot. Maybe he should have just turned up at Hammerstone's wearing a stupid hood.

'They should pay him by cheque', Jonny scoffs. 'That'd fuck him up, wouldn't it? You can just see him walking into Barclays trying to get a cheque cashed in the name of *The Great Mondo*.'

This loosens Evan up. He chuckles. 'Yeah, first name, *"The"*.'

Bobi Ofey comes in from the shower room, naked but for his unlaced boots. 'Hey Jonny, there's a copper looking for you.'

Jonny answers while trying to ignore the white elephant in the room. Or, more accurately, the swinging black dick.

'A copper? *Fuck*!'

Evan draws again and scrutinises Jonny through a cloud of his own making. 'Wotcha done now, Jonny?'

'I've got a bag of Nicky's films here, waiting to be picked up, and now I've got the Gestapo on my back.'

Upstairs, in the screening room above one of Nicky's book shops—the striptease place on Brewer Street—Nicky paces the floor, puffing on an Embassy and awaiting the verdict of the old ex-colonel who sits in the darkened room before a screen showing one of Nicky's masterpieces. It's a three-way featuring his wife going at it with another girl and his new 'rising star', Tough Taffy.

The Colonel's verdict is delivered thus. 'Have you got anything with bigger dicks?'

The man was taking the piss. Taffy had the biggest todger this side of Tiger Bay! This old bastard was as greedy as his entitled upbringing suggested.

Alan from downstairs poked his head round the curtains. 'Nick, there's a phone call for ya.'

Nicky threads another film through the spool, runs it and tells the old man, 'Hang on, Colonel, I got a call. Back in a jiffy.'

Nicky follows Alan down into the holiest of holy's—to a small room in the back where a couple of sleazoids are inspecting packets of eight-by-tens—the proper stuff; the dirt that's costing Nicky £800 a month to keep out of reach of the real filth. He follows Alan out into the respectable facade of the shop and grabs the phone behind the counter.

Alan serves another sucker with a couple of sealed '*blurred out pudenda*' books.

Nicky checks his suspect Rolex and necks the blower. He always checks the time when he takes a call. Timelines can prove significant. 'Yeah?'

It's Jonny.

'Nick, it's me. That cunt hasn't turned up yet and—.'

Nicky hears some kerfuffle on the other end of the line.

The Corn Exchange manager appears suddenly at his office door. 'What are you doing in here?'

'Hang on Nick—' Jonny necks the phone and addresses the manager. 'Dreaming of a white Christmas. What's it look like?' Jonny speaks back into the phone. 'He hasn't turned up, and guess what?'

The manager will not be ignored. 'You're not supposed to be in here!'

Jonny necks it again. 'Look, can I just make this call?'

'*I* happen to be the manager of this venue, and this is my office.'

'I'll be *two minutes*. Just let me—'

The manager tries to grab the receiver. 'No!'

Jonny pushes him away and tries again to speak into the receiver. 'Can't fuckin' believe this—I'm getting grief from the manager now!'

Nicky can hear the sound of a struggle on the other end of the line. 'What's up Jon?!'

Jonny holds the manager down in the middle of the floor with a double wrist lock and head scissors. He frees a hand and grabs the receiver again. The manager is screaming blue murder.

'Will you shut the fuck up! Christ! Nicky, I got a serious problem up here. Your boy hasn't turned up, and I got the fuckin' cops on my arse.'

'*Wait a minute, cop or cops?*'

'Fuckin' difference does it make?!'

'*Cop or cops?!*'

'I don't know. All I know is that there's a cop asking for me.'

Nicky chuckles, knowingly.

'This ain't funny, you cunt. I'm gonna get fuckin' pinched here!'

Nicky holds the phone away from his ear, enjoying the cacophony of Jonny's ranting and the manager screaming in the background. He beckons Alan over. 'Al, listen to this.'

Alan puts his ear to the phone. 'Satisfied or unsatisfied customer?'

'Jonny, Jonny,' Nicky pleads. 'Will you just fuckin' relax?!'

Alan shushes him and gestures to the handful of customers in the shop. Expletives issued in an establishment that deals in under-the-counter filth? Not on *Alan's* watch.

Nicky turns to the wall and takes it down a notch. 'Will you just relax?! Now listen . . .'

Ten minutes later, a Worsley police car pulls up next to Jonny's borrowed Cortina in the near-deserted car park behind the venue. Evan is in the passenger seat, blowing nervous smoke through the wound-down window.

A uniformed officer gets out of the Worsley. Jonny gets Nicky's bag out of the boot and hands it over.

Despite himself, Jonny bristles at the sight of a uniform these days. Iron bars and surreptitious Wormwood wanks loom large.

Without a word, the officer places the case on the bonnet of his car, unzips the bag and takes a brief look inside. Satisfied, and without a single word, takes the bag, gets in his car and drives out of the carpark; taillights fading in the Doncaster night.

Jonny gets behind the wheel of the Cortina and says, '*That* was Derek.'

12. BOOMERANG BARB

Ex body-builder, Sean Connery and a dyed-blonde Robert Shaw are making a convincing show of a dirty scrap in a train compartment. Connery pulls Shaw's jacket down over his arms, pulls him down and knees him neatly in the face.

Woah!

Nice move.

Jonny, Evan and Damien are among the crowd of the Streatham Odeon, thrilling at Connery's second outing as Ian Fleming's fighting, fucking secret agent, James Bond.

Bond and the girl gondola their way into the sunset on a Venetian waterway. Bond studies the dirty film that the Russians made of him and the girl earlier through a two-way mirror, and throws the unwound spool into the water as the end credits come up.

The boys re-enact the train fight among the throngs as they make their way out onto an early evening high road. Passers-by leap out of the way to avoid them as they throw each other around the street.

'Fuckin' grow up, you berks!', yells an old man, trying to get to his Morris Minor.

Evan breaks away from Damien's ham-fisted Front Headlock and makes for the White Lion just up the way. 'Right. Pub!'

'No,' Jonny says. 'Let's eat.'

The boys find an Italian place a few doors up. There are only a few other couples in there.

Evan and Damien have lasagne and beer. Jonny has crab and lemon tagliolini with white wine.

In between hearty gulps, Jonny waxes lyrical about the Porno Tony visit in Brixton a few weeks back.

'You know that day at Vern's, when I went with Nicky for that drive? Well, we were going over to his camera shop, but we stopped at what I thought was a mate of his. I left the room for a piss and when I came back, Nicky was in the process of stabbing this bloke in the face. I mean, one minute they're completely alright—talking about whatever—next minute, wham! I couldn't fucking believe what I was seeing.'

Evan considers this, scratching his chin. 'Stabbed him in the face?'

'Straight in the boat. I mean, it's not like I haven't seen anyone stabbed before—I've been stabbed myself—but it was the way it came outta no-where, wham!'

Damien's words wrestle around the food he's trying to swallow. 'You've been stabbed?'

Jonny places his cutlery neatly on either side of his plate, stands up, undoes his belt and pulls the left side of his trousers partly down, revealing a nasty gash just below the belt line.

Evan and Damien exclaim in unison. '*Fuck*!'

'That was my old man, that was.'

Damien examines the injury with morbid interest. 'Your dad did that?'

'Yeah. Fuckin' nut.'

'I think I'd rather be shot than stabbed', Damien muses.

A young waitress approaches the table. 'Could you not do that?' She gestures around the room as if there's a crowd watching.

Jonny pulls up his trousers. 'Do what?'

The waitress averts her eyes and walks away. 'Whatever it is you're doing.'

'Great,' Jonny says. 'Now she thinks we're queers.'

They all laugh as the waitress glares at them whilst tidying another table.

The chef, moustachioed, graven and unshaven—probably doing the waitress—appears at the serving hatch and gives them what they assume is *his look*.

Jonny returns it with his own and calls over. 'Have I got something you want?'

'Don't start now.' Evan is anxious to avoid a situation. 'Let's pay up and split before that cunt gives us a reason.'

The boys leave and head back to the cinema where Damien left his car. His assessment of Jonny issues forth. 'You're a fuckin' aggro magnet, you know that? Everywhere we go—'

'I tell you, Dame,' Jonny counters, 'back in Brynmawr, if we went out on a Friday night without chinning someone, the evening was considered a dead loss. Copping for a Donald was a consolation prize.'

'Failing that, there's always them sheep.'

'Fuck off.'

'How come your old man stabbed ya?'

'Actually, we stabbed each other. We had these knives on the kitchen wall that he brought back from when he was a prisoner of war with the "cold water taps". It was over a fucking Gene Vincent record that I bought in town. I put it on, and he went fucking ape shit. He grabbed a knife—I grabbed a knife, and it all kicked off. Later on, me Mam—she didn't know—was serving dinner, and me and the old bastard are sitting there pretending to be alright, but the two of us are fuckin' bleeding to death—'

Unison. Again. '*Fuck*!'

'—eventually we both passed out and when I came round, I was in hospital, and he was in the next bed. As soon as we saw each other, the fight kicked off again right there in the emergency ward. There were doctors sticking fuckin' needles in us and everything.'

The boys share incredulous laughter.

'He came down to visit me a couple of months ago and we fought then as well. I'm fucking telling you—a maniac, my old man.'

They reach Damien's Herald; get in and pull out on to the high street.

'Wrong way!' Evan warns.

'Is it?' Damien drives on, looking for a way to turn round.

'Another time—' Jonny continues, 'the crazy fucker got a couple of his mates from the pit to jump me on the way home to cut my sideburns off. Can you fuckin' believe that?'

'Fuckin' mad', Evan agrees.

Something across the street grabs Jonny by the eyes. 'Hang on.'

Evan follows his eye line and sees a row of closed shops. 'What?'

'Over there. That's Nicky's shop.'

'Which, what, where?'

'Over there. *Streatham Photographic*. Nicky's place.'

Damien pulls over outside the shop and the boys get out. Parked on the kerb is Nicky's Galaxie.

The boys gather around it.

'He must be here,' says Jonny.

Damien walks around the car: kicks the tires as if he's considering buying it. 'Where does he get these fucking things?'

'American connections, apparently,' Jonny informs him.

'Imagine trying to get that thing down Berwick Street. What happened to his Zodiac?'

'Have you ever known Nicky to keep the same car for more than a month?' Evan answers. He peers through the shop window into darkness. 'There's a light on somewhere.'

He locates a bell above the door and rings it.

Jonny says, 'Have you seen those films of his?'

Evan, still peering into the void, says, 'Has anyone *not* seen those films of his?'

Damien says, 'He's probably making one now.'

Evan comes away from the void. 'You reckon?'

Nicky comes creeping down a side alley, holding a cricket bat. He hides in the shadows until he identifies the visitors. 'Oh, it's *you* cunts.'

Evan sees him first. 'Well, we were just in the neighbourhood'

'Come 'round back. I'm just finishing up.'

They follow Nicky to the back of the shop and down a narrow staircase. The studio is dimly lit and warm. At one end of the basement is a large white back-drop, surrounded by lamps on stands. Clearly, a session has recently taken place.

Nicky walks around, turning off the lamps. 'Bit out of your jurisdiction, ain't it? Streatham. Whatchu doin' on the wrong side of the drink?'

Jonny admires the rows of drying photos hung across the room like pornographic bunting. 'We've just been to see that new James Bond film.'

Nicky flips on his jacket. 'Whatcha think?'

'Good. He has this great fight on a train with this Russian spy . . . proper scrap.'

'Yeah, me and the missus saw it the other day. All she could go on about was the bit where they secretly film Bond and that bird shagging through a two-way mirror. Said they should've shown that bit instead of panning away. Couldn't stop going on about what positions they probably fucked in. Nutty cow.'

'Sounds like quite a girl,' Damien says.

'She is that.'

Evan picks up a camera. Peers through the lens and weighs it in his hand. 'You should be careful with these things: they've been known to cause photography.'

Nicky bags some films and zips up. 'Whatchu boys doin' now?'

'Dropping these cunts off and going home', Damien says.

'No, you're not. Fuck that. We're going out. My treat. Gotta swing by the house first.' Nicky frantically searches his jacket pockets. 'Where did I leave my fuckin' fags . . . ah!' He pulls the pack from an inside pocket and sparks up. 'You know that Sean Connery's bald as a coot, doncha?'

Jonny hates to see the mighty demolished. 'Bollocks.'
'Straight up. It's a syrup.'
'Bollocks.'

Evan says, 'You making another film?'

'Photos. Have a look, they're hanging in there.'

Evan does as he's directed. 'Fuckin' 'ell. Have a butcher's!'

The boys join Evan in the side room. Wet glossies pegged to a line depict a woman totally encased in rubber, including a gas mask and cape.

Evan takes a close look. 'What the fuck are these?'

Nicky drags hard. Exhales soft. 'Miriam. You should've got here earlier. You could have met her. The bird sparks. Goes like a belt-fed mortar.'

Evan backs off, as if he might catch something. 'My missus would lose her shit if she knew I was even looking at this stuff. It's just weird. I don't get it.'

Jonny is inclined to agree. 'That has got to be the creepiest thing I ever seen.'

Nicky pontificates. When he's in the mood, he's the pope of pontification. He's in the mood now.

'Gettin' off is less a matter of frottage and more a matter of the psyche: where your head is at. You want a cosmic orgasm, boys, it's up here,' he points, loaded gun-like at his head, 'not here'. He thumbs down towards the front of his trousers. 'Anyone can ejaculate, but it takes a higher state of mind to truly escalate—to attain the quasi-religious experience that a proper fuck should be.'

'Tuh! You can ram your quasi-religious experiences and cosmic orgasms,' Jonny answers. 'A normal orgasm does me just fine.'

The boys concur with vague nods. None of them really know what the fuck they're discussing. Even Jonny.

Nicky regards the trio with bemusement. 'You idiots don't know what you're missing.'

Ten minutes later, Nicky and Damien's cars crawl towards a large house in a quiet leafy suburb. Nicky hops out, pushes the big wrought-iron gates open, jumps back in the car and leads a motorcade of two up the gravel driveway.

The hallway light is on.

Nicky shouts up the stairs, 'Barb!'

No answer.

Nicky leads everyone into a large lounge.

Part art gallery—part discotheque.

Plush.

Stylish.

So much so, it feels like an infraction to be in it.

Over in the corner is a small bar, in marbled red and finished with gold piping. A stylistic anomaly, as virtually everything else in the room is either black or white.

Damien admires a creepy framed painting of skeletons waiting in a train station.

Nicky stands beside him, re-igniting the effect of the picture anew through Evan's uninitiated eyes. 'Paul Devaux. Belgian surrealist. Fake, but a good one. The missus loves this shit.'

'Fucking lovely place, Nick. What a gaff!'

'I use the same designer as Peter Sellers,' Nicky declares. 'A nasty cunt he is, Sellers.'

Jonny is taken with the wall-wide display of swords and knives, which remind him of the two Jap daggers his dad had at home. Nicky's collection boasts Gurkha Kukris, an Arabian scimitar, a couple of Nazi daggers and the star of the show . . . a 40-inch Samurai Katana. The ivory sheath and handle are intricately carved with renderings of figures of Jap mythology and dragons in clouds. Jonny basks in its presence and vows right then to have one just like it one day.

Nicky breaks the spell. 'Have any of you tried marijuana?'

Not Evan. 'Never heard of her.'

Neither has Jonny. 'Who?'

"*Who?*" Nicky scoffs. 'Y'fuckin' squares.'

Marijuana is not on the boy's collective lexicon. The boys convey puzzlement.

Nicky shall amend this. 'Sort yourselves out a drink. Bar's over there. I'll go and roll one for us. Back in a jiffy.'

Nicky leaves them to it and goes upstairs.

Evan goes straight behind the bar. 'Right. Wot we got 'ere den? Jonny?'

'Has he got any Mateus?'

'*Mateus*!? Have beer, you stuck up cunt! Dame? Beer?'

'Yeah.'

Evan raids the bar and hands out the drinks.

Jonny is all about the décor . . . Nicky's paintings, statuettes and weapons . . . He swigs the beer, puts the bottle to one side and continues to admire. 'What was he on about?' Mari-what?'

Evan stands with him and shares Jonny's admiration. 'Fuck knows . . . and all that bollocks about a *higher state of ejaculation* or whatever. He sounds like one o' them American psychologist twats.'

Damien spots the big wooden Phillips dancetté by the bay window and shouts up the staircase. 'Nick!? Can we put some music on?'

Nicky shouts back. '*Yeah, there's some of the wife's records in the thing under the window.*'

Damien goes to the state-of-the-art radiogram, with its sliding glass doors, and pulls out a handful of LPs, most of it Jazz bollocks. 'What the fuck is a *Thelonious Monk*, for fuck's sake?' He finds one with an unrecognisable (without glasses) Buddy Holly on the cover. He puts it on. 'Here's one for you, Jonny.'

As the opening chords of *I'm Gonna Love You Too* chimes loudly from a single speaker, the grumbling of a car engine outside on the driveway chokes off.

Someone enters the hallway and makes their way straight upstairs. A woman's voice, with a taint of an American accent, calls the house. 'Nick, where are you?'

The boys exchange glances. Do *we* answer?

Nicky shouts down, '*Up here!*'

Evan steps outside the room in time to see the woman's long legs and shapely behind ascending the stairs. He steps back into the room and thumbs upwards. 'The *arse* on that.'

Barbara Nash finds Nicky in the bedroom, sitting on the edge of the bed, rolling a tight joint—tongue, lizard-like—coating the edge of the Rizla paper.

'Who's here?'

'Some of the boys from Hammerstone's.'

Barbara Nash is a Beatnik's wet dream, red wool jacket with a black fur collar, tight black turtleneck sweater, slacks and suede pixie boots. A full carrot-top of hair cascades, Bardot-like, over her pockmarked cheek; a thick black hairband making sense of it all.

She goes to the multi-mirrored dressing table, opens the drawer, takes out a small vial of capsules, pops one, and puts the vial in her jacket pocket.

He up and downs her. 'Where you bin?'

'Chaz's'

'Richardson? Not *those* cunts. I told you I don't like you going over there. I urge respectable distance when it comes to that lot.'

'The guy fainted before they got started, anyway. I think he had a heart attack.'

'Anticipation can do that.' He twists the end of the joint and bites it off. 'Did he die?'

'Don't know. He didn't look too clever when they dragged him out.'

'Anyone we know?'

'No. I never seen him before.'

'Keep an ear out for who it was. Might be worth knowing somewhere down the road.'

Nicky sparks the joint, drags long, places it in the ashtray and moves up behind her. He reaches around to cup her maybe too-heavy-for-her-slender-frame breasts. Without turning round, she reaches down behind her and squeezes his crotch. She takes his hand and pushes it down under the front of her slacks ... under her knickers ...

He finds her and circles accordingly.

She pushes her hips forward into his fingers, her shoulders into his chest. 'Oh, you fucker' She gasps and staggers forward, steadies herself against the dresser ... *'You fucker'*

She's always been quick off the trigger. No fucking around with this girl.

Nicky flips a few tissues from the box on the dresser, wipes his hand and retrieves the neglected joint. He drags again and hands it to her.

She sits in front of the dresser and watches herself in the three mirrors as she drags, long and slow, glowing delightedly in a triptych of post-orgasm serenity

'We're going out,' Nicky tells her. 'Come with. Meet the boys.'

The boys have taken seats now. They lounge and drink and chat and admire, with Buddy Holly still hiccupping out of the dancetté. Look at this place! Whatever Nicky's game is, he wins at it.

It hits Evan first. 'You smell that?'

Jonny and Damien *No* in unison. Nicky comes down the stairs, enters and offers the joint to Damien, who's sitting nearest. 'Have a bang on that.'

Damien takes it, studies it, sniffs it. 'What is it?'

'It's a joint, numb nuts. Smoke it like a fag. But go easy.'

Damien does as directed, tentatively, and eyes Nicky through squinty lids. Nicky carefully removes the joint from Damien's fingers and offers it to Jonny.

'I told ya, I don't smoke.'

'It's not a fag.'

'Don't care. It's that shit the blacks smoke over in Kensal. It stinks.'

'Square.'

'Fuck off, triangle.'

Evan steps in. 'Ere.'

Jonny keeps his distance as the rest puff and cough, and laugh and puff, and cough again.

Barbara Nash appears at the doorway, watching the scene. One by one, the boys acknowledge this fresh presence.

Maybe the loaded air slows time down, so it takes a while to properly remember her.

Maybe they think this funny cigarette is making them hallucinate. That would explain it.

Maybe this funny cigarette induces déjà vu and only makes them *think* she is some kind of reoccurrence.

Maybe, baby...

Nicky makes the intros: 'Everybody, this is Barbara... the wife. Barb... this is a bunch of poofs that jump around in their pants for a living.'

Polluted lungs aside, if anyone could have afforded a gasp, they would have done, as everyone recognises Jonny's knee trembler from the Locarno.

Remember?

The night Jonny got twatted in Catford by Kelly Hewitt?

The night they tried to cheer Jonny up by getting him pissed at the Locarno.

The night Jonny and the girl, now standing before them, skipped off to the ladies for a quick Donald Duck while the boys took the piss out of Liv and Marina at the bar.

The night Jonny fucked the stylish beatnik who now stands before them at Nicky Nash's lounge-way door... all married and that... to Nicky Nash.

Jonny does.

Oh, you fucker...

You'd think that winding that night up by chinning a copper in Soho and ending up in the clinker would be about as bad as that night got.

But no.

It looms large.

Large enough to encompass *this* evening six months later.

Of course, the collective agony escapes the bespectacled one. Or does it? Jonny's hope that Mrs Nash won't remember him is immediately scuppered. Loaded mutual recognition connects them to *their* moment.

She twigs alright and declares it surreptitiously with a wry smirk.

Nicky takes a final drag, stubs the soggy dog-end in the ashtray, and whips out his car keys. 'Right, let's go!'

13. CROSSFIRE

They were in Albertopolis now.
 South Kensington.
 Ponse country.
Where the museums are.
The *right* end of Kensington.

The boys share an unspoken query. What the fuck did Nicky want to come here for?

They arrive in a three-car motorcade of Nicky's Galaxie, Damien's Herald, and Barbara's little red Triumph Spitfire. In the backseat of Damien's car, Jonny ponders the chances of getting everyone to go to the 2i's instead, but then that shitty folk band skiffles into his mind's eye, so he jettisons the idea. But geography and Rock 'n' Roll's submission to this new wave of 'teacher music' is not the chief concern now. The chief concern is Barbara Nash and that half-forgotten Locarno knee trembler's unwelcome return on Jonny's radar. If this evening proves to contain a big reveal, Jonny should be there when it happens.

The Cromwellian Club is a converted regency building, ornate of architecture, high of ceiling and grand of scale—a nightclub version of that talent scout, Jerry Pro's apartment.

Under sparkling chandeliers, they enter a large reception room, which leads off into a casino and a dance floor, from where Johnny Kidd & the Pirates' latest hit blares loud. Jonny dismisses the possibility that the disk jockey is playing it just for him. Yeah, he was on the up and up but not quite *that* famous. Yet...

Everyone seems to know someone, so disperse to catch up with thick thieves and cunty acquaintances.

Jonny knows no-one, so finds the bar, orders a gin with ice and scans the crowded dance floor. There she is— Barbara Nash—doing the twist or some variation of whatever the current craze dictates. She can dance, he'd give that. And by extension, can probably fuck too. Couldn't really go by the Locarno encounter: her with one foot up on the bowl, arms steading herself against either wall, and him just hardly started. If he'd given it any thought at the time, he'd assume her enthusiasm was also booze-fuelled. But looking at her now? The way she moves ...

Barbara Nash can fuck. You can see that by the way her hips lock into the beat and goes with it—that given half a chance she'd ruin a bloke wonderfully.

'I'll never get over you ...' sings the patched-eyed Pirate.

Great.
Nicky's bird.
No.
Strike that.
Nicky's fucking *wife*.

'She don't do nothing without my say so. She knows what'll fuckin' happen if she did.'

Old four eyes has done him a solid with the car, and for that Jonny is grateful and quite enjoying his new found solvency thank you very much. But should things ever escalate to a violent vis-à-vis with the bloke? Jonny knows the man is tasty, but having never seen him in action without a blade (or a sausage roll), he has few doubts that the bespectacled one can be bested, blade or no blade. But it wouldn't end there, would it? Jonny would find himself in vendetta country forevermore and would need to keep an eye out for the criminal cavalry behind Nicky Nash.

Well, I Ask You, Eden Kane's swaggering diatribe comes on.

Nicky barges through the crowd of first-degree poseurs, ponces and half-cut celebs to the other end of the bar, waves a twenty and a barman is on him.

'Right ... a Guinness, three bitters ...'

'Pints?'

'Pints, yeah. A Cinzano; two Vodkas and coke; and a glass of red. Quick as you can.'

The barman dodges in and out of the other bar staff, collecting the drinks. He places them one by one on a tray in front of Nicky until he has them all. 'That's eh . . . 8 and 6, 8 and 6, 8 and 6. Vodka, coke . . . That's two pounds and eighteen shillings, please.'

Nicky peels off a note and is about to hand it over. But something is wrong. 'Hang on . . . where's the Advocaat?'

'Did you say Advocaat?'

'Yeah, yeah. Advocaat. Yeah.'

'K.' Hang on.'

The moment the barman turns to get the missing drink, Nicky pockets his money, grabs the tray, and disappears into the crowd.

Liv and Marina are here, dancing with Barbara and some of the other girls. Even Doreen and the one-armed-bandit are over there. Wherever the wrestlers are, they are.

Evan has gone for a piss and Damien has seen Atomic Twin, Lincoln Borge, and has gone over to talk to him.

Barbara sees Jonny drinking his gin alone by the bar and goes over. 'Hi Jonny,' she sings teasingly.

'Hello,' Jonny responds, flatly.

'So, you're one of the wrestlers.'

Jonny has to admit, it's wonderful to be able to answer yeah in all honesty, 'Yeah.'

'Well,' she winks, 'you certainly showed me a few holds.'

Jonny throws a quick glance around the noisy, crowded room to ensure no-one catches his answer. 'Alright, *mouth*. Pipe down. What's wrong with you?!'

'I won't say anything if you don't.' She sidles up, closer. The way she does it reminded him of those tarts in Tisbury Court that had so rattled his dad.

'It'll be our little secret.'

She mimes that mouth zipping-and-lock thing and throws the invisible key over her shoulder.

'Sounds good to me. Let's never speak of it again.'

Jonny is intrigued by that slight American twang in her voice, but thinks better of expressing his interest.

'Your friends know though, right?'

'Course not!' Jonny lies. Or does he? What they may or may not remember from that night has never been properly discussed. All they knew for sure was Jonny's vacating the establishment fast.

'Why not? Liv and Marina know.'

'Who?'

Barbara holds up her Cinzano by way of a toast to her girls on the dancefloor. Liv sees her, winks, and waves back. 'Liv and Marina, they were there. Remember?'

'Jonny struggles to recollect. Much remains missing from that fateful night. 'I don't remember 'em.'

'Yeah. Well, we didn't mess around, did we?' she giggles. 'I think we understood each other pretty fast, huh?'

'What can I say?' Jonny smiles, sardonically. 'The night remains a blur.'

She giggles again and feigns a thick English accent. 'Tell it to the judge, m'lud.'

Jonny scans the room, quick. Nicky is nowhere to be seen. 'My mates'll keep their gobs shut,' Jonny stage-whispers. 'You better hope your lot do the same.'

'Don't worry, they'll keep schtum. But I'm not so sure about yours. Nicky says that if you want a secret to get around quick, tell a wrestler. Right little sewing circle, those guys, Nicky reckons.'

'Does he?'

'But it's not me Nicky'll kill if it does get around.'

'She don't do nothing without my say so. She knows what'll fuckin' happen if she did.'

Jonny doesn't entertain threats, and this sounds just like one.

'Look you, Nicky ain't killing no one. But there's no need for things to hit that pitch. And let's get one thing straight. I'm not scared of him or any other fucker.'

'Maybe you should be, Jonny. It's a wicked world.'

'Well, I'm not. I'm well aware of his reputation—about Henry and all that.'

'Henry?'

Jonny knows he's misspoken. 'Henry... did I say Henry? I meant... Eric.'

'No, c'mon, who's Henry?'

'For fuck's sake. I meant Eric. Eric Overman.'

'See what I mean? *Mouth*. I hope your friends are better liars than you are. I'll ask him about Henry later—'

Jonny's open hands go to fists. 'You'll shut yer fuckin' trap!'

'Ooooooh! You're even *more* fuckable when you're angry.'

Jonny has overplayed, and he knows it. Worse: *she* knows it. The future, immediate and distant, has just dimmed a notch.

Ignorant of the temper, Nicky approaches with the tray of stolen drinks and sets them on a table. He looks around for the boys and summons them over.

Evan, Damien and Jonny gather round and avoid eye contact. Mutual agony is a place where Barbara reigns like a queen. This is fun.

A very mellow Nicky Nash hands out the drinks. 'Ere you go... ere' you go...'

'Hey, Nicky!' Someone recognises him and comes bounding over. 'Alright, Nick. How's it going?'

It's Superintendent Basil Zwick: firmly in Eric and Peter's pocket, but fraternising with the filth in public is less than intelligent, no matter *how* in the pocket the fraternisers might be. The appearance of this balding, tuxedoed fool, with some little big titted dolly on his arm, is a rude interruption. The rest of the boys know a copper when they see one and casually drift away. This exodus is an annoyance and eradicates much of whatever mellow Nicky had on board. He was feeling good and in a *holding court* kind of a mood. Dischuffed is now the order of the moment.

'Oh . . . alright Baz,' Nicky responds dryly. 'How's it going?'

'I saw you the other day, and you walked right past me.'

'Did I?'

'Yeah, you were coming out of the arcade in Coldharbour Lane. You looked right at me but didn't say a thing.'

'Basil, I obviously didn't see you, mate.'

'I thought, you ignorant cunt.' The man haw haws.

'I didn't see you, but *you* saw me. Why didn't *you* say hello?'

'Well, you didn't say nothing so—'

Nicky's angry now. He glances at the nervous dolly at the Superintendent's side. But fuck her. 'What Am I, the fuckin' oracle of all greetings?'

'Woah woah! Easy, Nick—'

'I'll tell you what, next time you see me, do me a favour. Say hello and I'll fuckin' knock you out, you cunt. Now fuck off.'

The Superintendent sputters some; looks at his date. All reasonable responses escape him. Leading the girl by her bare arm, he scurries away, stunned.

Jonny and Barbara come back to the table.

Nicky mutters to no one in particular. 'Wreck *my* buzz, the cunt.'

Jonny watches the hapless Superintendent bustle his way into the crowd. 'Close, were ya?'

'Ah, fuck 'im.' Nicky shouts after the harried Superintendent for good measure. 'Baz! Basil!'

Basil and his girl turn around.

'Fuck off!'

Basil shakes his head. They continue on their way.

'There's your drink there, Jon . . . Barb?'

They take their drinks.

Jonny swigs.

Barbara sips.

'Right,' Nicky announces, 'piss time!' And off he goes to have one.

Barbara watches him go and slips a tiny glass vial into Jonny's hand.

'Here, I think you could do with a livener.'

Jonny studies it in full view of anyone who may care to look.

Barbara pushes his hand down out of sight. 'Get clever!'

Jonny knows not what he holds. 'What is it?'

'What do you *think*? If you're going to take one, be discrete.'

'What is it, drugs?'

'Yeah, Drinamyl.'

Jonny shoves it back at her. She catches it against her generous chest.

'You won't catch me taking that shit. Is that what you two are on? Stoned, are ya? That's what they call it, ain't it? Stoned? Is that why you're both acting the cunt?'

'He don't need it. He's a natural.'

'*Charming*. Charming way to talk about your husband. What's your excuse, then?'

'As you say, I'm stoned, baby! Stoned as an Arab adulteress.'

The evening has taken on a nightmarish hue, and Jonny wonders what buses are still running that might deliver him from it.

'Look,' Barbara says, soothingly. 'Let's be friend's, eh? Truce?'

She holds out a slender hand to shake. Jonny regards it for a moment as if it was as mysterious an object as that vial of speed he'd just thrown at her. He ignores it and slugs the last of his gin.

Over by the record booth, Damien is talking to "Atomic Twin" Lincoln. '. . . Yeah, I was pretty fucked off that I couldn't make it to the funeral. Was it a big do?'

Damien knows not. He wasn't there and says so. 'So I'm told. I couldn't make it either.'

'I should think Jock and Gil were there, though, to represent the boys, like.'

'Yeah, I would have thought so.'

Both boys toast their fallen comrade with warm beers. *'Dominic Farrago!'*

Lincoln breaks the three-second silence. 'Who're you here with tonight? Cheryl? How is she? How *is* the wife?'

Mrs Cheryl Logan would be none too chuffed if she knew her husband was pissing it up in South Ken. Especially as she thinks he's still a Hammerstone wrestler and fighting in Bristol tonight.

'No, I'm with some of the boys, Nicky and Evan. Tarzan's over there somewhere as well.'

'Nicky who? Not Nash?!'

'Yeah. He's here with his missus. I'll tell you something funny about that later.'

'He's *here*? *Where*? They're all after him—'

'He's right over there somewhere. Whotchu on about? Who's after him?'

Lincoln gets earnest. 'You know who's running this place now, right?'

'No.'

'"Rich" Clifford.'

'Sherman's running *this* ponse palace? Since when?'

'Since now. A whole bunch of faces, north and south, have been warring over the place for months. Seems to have landed in Sherman's lap for the time being.' Lincoln points to somewhere across the room. 'And you see that thing over there . . . the hostess in that purple dress carry on?'

Damien sees who he's talking about. A looker, but one who's pretty much had her day, laughing and theatrically winking at something some punter is flapping on about.

'Yeah, Wanda.'

'You know her?'

'Tits-arse-hair-Wanda? Everyone knows tits-arse-hair-Wanda.'

'Right, but here's your starter for ten and no conferring. What's tits-arse-hair-Wanda's maiden name? Here's a clue. It begins with *Sher* and ends with *man*.'

'Okay, so Wanda's Clifford's—'

'*Sister*. Did you hear about that little row Nicky had with her Tony in Brixton the other day?'

'*Porno* Tony! Fuck. We were just talking about that.'

'Right, so was *Wanda*, to her vicious fat poof of a brother.' Lincoln scans the raucous room. 'Her Tony's here as well, somewhere. I think ol' four-eyes has just walked into an ambush.'

Damien weighs it. 'I know he had a go at someone called Tony, but I didn't know it was *Porno* Tone.' He knocks back the last of his bitter. 'I'd better find him and get him out of here.'

Billy Fury's *Halfway to Paradise* comes on.

Back over at the entrance, Barbara's wind-up continues. 'So, you on the pull tonight, then?'

'I'm out having a drink, that's all,' Jonny replies firmly.

'Married?'

Jonny body-swerves the question and delivers what he expects to be his knockout punch. 'I think I've seen one of your little films. What a class act.'

'Oh yeah, which one?'

'Out in the woods somewhere.'

'Well, there's nothing like an alfresco fuck with a nice breeze on your ass.'

The girl is bullet proof.

Calvary arrives—Damien shaped. 'Have you seen Nick?'

The bullet-proof Mrs Nash nods towards the dancefloor. 'Probably out there in the erection section.'

The grand stone staircase with its wrought iron balustrades seems to embrace the marbled reception area beneath the chandeliers and feature fireplaces. Out here, the heavy oak doors muffle Billy Fury's strident lament.

Nicky comes out of the toilets onto the upstairs hallway and walks straight into Wanda Sherman—a rude awakening of purple satin and Pris Presley hair.

She wants a word. 'I want a word with you, Nash.'

'Oh yeah, about what, I wonder?'

'You *know* about what.'

'No, I *don't* know about what. Say your piece, or piece off.'

'You know Cliff's running this place now, don't you?'

Nicky grabs the woman's face, squeezing her cheeks together, and pushes her head hard against the marbled wall. 'Don't threaten me, tart. I've been threatened by professionals—and no—I didn't know Clifford was running this place. But I do know he's a fuckin' fairy, and I do know he'd be none too chuffed with you or your ponce of a boyfriend if he was privy to your little day job in Dean Street. You readin' me?'

He shoves her aside and heads back to the ballroom. Someone hovers in his peripheral. It's Porno Tony, standing at the top of the stairs with a big plaster across his left check. Silly sod doesn't know whether to shit himself or turn into a pumpkin.

Nicky sneers at Wanda, then strides over to confront her boyfriend. 'The episode is over, Tone. You wanna make a fuckin' ongoing series of it or what?'

Tony turns his freshly patched up cheek towards Nicky. 'Look what you fucking did to me, Nick—'

As Tony jabbers nervously, he slips on the highly polished steps and tumbles down the curved stairway and lands on his head in the foyer. The dolled up and be-suited all turn to see Nicky descending the staircase, giggling dementedly and holding his hands up in a I-*never-touched-him-honest* surrender.

Two dickie-bowed bouncers, Les and Stanley, come in from the entrance to help Tony up. 'I've done me ankle!' he wails.

Wanda looks down from the balcony.

Les conveys concern. 'Fuckin' 'ell, you alright mate?'

Nicky approaches and laughs his chokey laugh. 'I swear I never fuckin' touched him.'

As soon as Les and Stanley realise that this is Nicky Nash, they drop Tony on the floor and pile into him. Nicky fights dirty, biting, kicking and throwing metal ashtray stands. The two bouncers manoeuvre him into the back office, out of view of the in-coming clientele—sharp suited media types with their wives and mistresses.

The fight continues in the back room—a small office—until two of Sherman's top enforcers, Vince, Raymond, and the barman Nicky robbed earlier, barge in and help overpower the bespectacled one.

Wanda comes into the room, followed by the man himself, "Rich" Clifford Sherman, as Nicky is dragged up on to a chair where he is held by the four men.

The below-the-knee deep-red mohair coat with the black fur collar; the big sovereign ring; seconded by the diamond pinkie-ring, hints that Clifford Sherman might be just a little light in those snakeskin Italian loafers. What's left of his blonde hair is smarmed down with a tonic of mysterious marque over a pampered reddened face. Twinkling piggy eyes survey his captured prey, delightedly.

'Nicky Nash . . . *Flash* Nicky Nash.' Sherman speaks with the rich brogue of a BBC news presenter. '*Wildman of South West two*. Long-time no mayhem . . . Tut tut. Actually . . . that's not *quite* true, is it, Nick?'

Back out on the dance floor, Evan is engaged in a slow creep around with Marina. He enjoys the contours of her pubic region against his stiffening dick. She's had a few now—drinks, that is—and doesn't mind.

Damien interrupts the moment. 'Have you seen him?'

'Ah, fuck off. Not again!'

'Where the fuck is he?'

Evan outlines the most plausible narrative. 'He's obviously got wind of what's up and pissed off. Go and get a round in, you tight cunt.'

In the backroom, Sherman squares up to the man held down before him, removes the glasses and holds them up to the light. 'Fuckin' 'ell Nick, you must have good eyesight to see out of these.'

Sherman has made a joke. This means his goons will laugh accordingly. And they do.

What little humanity Nicky possesses is extinguished by this remark. His feeble eyes lock tight on Sherman like some predatory reptile.

Sherman wiggles the thick black horn rims back onto Nicky's face. 'You know, with a physique like yours, Nick, you can't afford to be hostile. You're really going to have to curb all this throwing your weight about ... certainly on this side of the river, anyway.' Sherman turns his back with a swish, and although still addressing Nicky, projects to the room. 'Would Henry be present, perchance?'

Sherman nods to Les, who rummages through Nicky's inside pockets and relieves him of *Henry*.

'Ah ... of course he would.'

Les hands *Henry* to Sherman, who holds it up for all to see, then switches the blade and runs it sensuously down Nicky's face. 'We're not yanks, Nick. Only wogs use these things over here.'

Nicky fixes the man before him with a locked and loaded glare. 'You know, on my side of the drink, you pull a blade on someone, you better follow through.'

'Nicky Nicky Nicky... nobody *wants* this aggro—'

'Ah go on, have some on me—'

Nicky jerks his head forward, sinking his teeth deep into Sherman's powdered wrist, causing the tip of the blade to pierce the hollow of Nicky's check. Startled, Sherman squeals and jumps back, dropping the switchblade to the tiled floor with a clatter. Nicky's teeth are still firmly embedded in Sherman's wrist.

Everyone in the room recoils.

Sherman screams.

Wanda screams.

Someone yells, 'Fuckin' maniac!'

Nicky seizes the moment, still holding Sherman's wrist in his mouth, brings his feet up into Sherman's stomach, kicks hard and propels himself backwards into the men behind him.

All three men hit the ground in a comedy kerfuffle. Nicky leaps to his feet and stomps Les and Stanley as they make clumsy grabs for him. Nicky lunges for the door. Instead of escaping through the foyer and outside, he runs up the stairs and back into the club.

Les, Stanley and Vince chase him with Sherman's order bellowing over the music. 'Just follow him! Don't kick off in here! Just get him out of here, quietly!'

Someone yells again, 'Fuckin' maniac!'

By now, Jonny, Evan, Damien, Barbara, Marina and Liv are sitting around a big table with a young actor, Joe, who they recognise from some hospital program off the telly, with his girlfriend.

Joe's a fan. He asks fan questions. '... but I thought you were all bitter enemies! When I saw you two at the Albert Hall, I genuinely thought you were trying to kill each other.'

Barbara strokes Jonny's leg under the table and pokes her tongue into her cheek, blowjob style.

Jonny conveys imperviousness.

But that's the point.

She knows this.

This is funny.

Calm and cold, Jonny hisses from the corner of his mouth, '*Will you fuck off?*'

Joe is still gushing . . . 'Don't you remember?' he says to his girl, 'This is *Damien Logan*, and this is *Evan Leigh!*'

The girl is intrigued. 'Don't you care if people know you're all friends?'

'Y'see,' Joe says, 'we thought you all hated each other.'

'Only when we get paid' says Evan.

'Anyone got thrupence?' Says Damien.

Everyone laughs except Jonny, who is pissed off with the boys for not keeping up the pretence of their mutual animosity, but even more pissed off over his not being well known enough to be recognised by semi-known actors in poncy clubs.

Barbara sidles up closer and whispers in Jonny's ear, 'Guess what I did today?'

'Don't know. Don't care.'

'Oh, you're no fun! Come on, guess.'

'Stopped being a twat for eight seconds?'

'Wrong.'

'There's no way around this, is there?' Jonny concedes. 'Go on then. What—*Mrs Nash*—did you do today?'

'Weeeeeeell . . . I saw a man have a heart attack.'

'Great. And?'

'Don't you want to know *why* he had a heart attack?'

'Something to do with you?'

'No.'

Jonny sighs big. 'So, cut to it, shall we?'

'Do you know the Richardsons?'

'The brothers?'

'Yeah. Chaz and Eddie.
'The torture squad?'
'Bingo!'

For the first time tonight, Jonny takes a good close-up look at Barbara Nash. Her pale face, as far as Jonny understood these things, was makeup free—all but a natural beauty if not for a complexion ravaged by a long-gone bout of severe acne. Jonny doubted that its partial obscuration by the red Bardot waves cascading over them was anything to do with reservations about her public image. As hip and stylish as she obviously was, Jonny suspected Barbara Nash operated on a level far above the petty dictates of vanity, and by that same token, not quite in possession of herself.

Her intense emerald eyes hold his attempted indifference lasciviously. It was the same look she cast upon him in the Locarno toilets. Only, he wasn't so indifferent then.

'They were just about to zap the guy, but he passed out as soon as they got out the jump cables.'

She sips her Cinzano and looks impishly around the room as if she'd playfully announced she was wearing no bra.

Jonny could make no sense of the statement. There was no coherent response to it. Whether it was true or not was beside the point. It was the kind of thing only a total head case would come out with. What do you say to the clearly unhinged?

As it turns out, he doesn't need to.

Nicky appears at the table, nursing his face with a bloodstained serviette.

Everyone recoils.

Everyone says 'Fuck!'

'Sit down,' Nicky orders. 'Relax.'

'What the fuck happened to you?!' Evan says.

Nicky stands there, in his black suit and thick horn-rims, mopping his bleeding face with the bloodstained napkin—

like a Dali rendering of a Japanese flag—surrounded by enemies and as cool as a puffin's bollocks.

'C'mon, Nick,' Damien urges. 'You need to get the fuck out of here.'

'Relax, I said.' Nicky holds the napkin away from his face and inspects the stains with detached interest. 'I'm gonna finish my drink and leave when I'm ready.'

He picks up his Guinness and toasts Sherman's men as they glare over the crowded ballroom from the exits. All they want to do is get him out of the place. There will be a reckoning at a later date one way or another, but *off* the premises.

What happens next would become the stuff of clubland mythology.

What is certain is that Barbara Nash calmly finishes her drink, and then indiscriminately throws her glass high over her shoulder behind her.

The glass shatters.

She grabs a bottle of someone else's wine and throws that over her shoulder, too.

It doesn't smash, but someone screams.

And that's all she wrote.

Like a starting pistol, The Shadows' *The Savage* roars out of the speaker system—a raucous, galloping guitar instrumental—which seems to ignite a melee of indiscriminate punches and vicious kicks.

Ashtrays and bottles come back in a wild arc.

Sherman's boys push and shoulder their way through the panicking crowd.

Nicky sees them closing in, ducks down under the table, lifts it, sending candelabras and buckets of ice everywhere, and runs with it—part shield, part battering ram—towards the approaching bouncers.

The room is a chaotic nightmare—answered with spraying blood and shattering glass. Everyone scrambles to get away from the epicentre of the mayhem, trampling over the unlucky ones who have stumbled to the ground.

Then shit went O.K. Coral.

The few people who are still on their feet hit the deck fast when two deafening gunshots go off.

BAM!

BAM!

Everyone searches their beings for bullet wounds.

Broken plaster and dust rain down from the ceiling, confirming shots fired high.

Some fool ducks and runs straight into Jonny, knocking him to the floor. As the bloke jumps over him, Jonny punches him in the balls. The man staggers sideways and bounces off the bar. Jonny leaps to his feet, ready for another round. The man stays put, clutching his meat rack as panic seizes the room.

Someone grabs Jonny around the neck and tries to wrestle him to the ground. Jonny lurches forward, reaches down, grabs the man's leg and pulls up hard. The back of the man's head hits the dancefloor, hard. Jonny stands over him: Sammy Fortnoy. Sherman's first lieutenant. Jonny almost laughs. Does this fool know what he's done? It seems not. Fortnoy, recognising Jonny now, leaps up with surrender hands. 'Jonny, sorry, *mate*! I didn't know it was you! Honest!'

James Bond's smooth move came to Jonny now. Sammy Fortnoy's frightened visage offers the perfect opportunity to see if it works. Jonny pulls the man's jacket down, leaving his arms trapped beside him. Jonny delivers a tight right hook, sending Fortnoy to wherever their receivers go.

Jonny takes too long, marvelling over the move's effectiveness.

Someone punches him in the face.

And before he can get his hands to the offender . . .

BAM!

That fucking gun!

Jonny throws himself backwards over the bar, quickly righting himself to assess the pandemonium and wonders whose arse he needs to stick that gun up.

That punch rings righteously below his right eye. He has to admit; it was a beaut. Across the room, with his good eye, he sees Nicky holding two champagne bottles, clubbing indiscriminately, like a hoodlum Custer, surrounded by tux-clad Cheyenne warriors.

Above the mayhem, up on the balcony, through the nicotine fog and gun smoke, stands Barbara Nash, looking down with rapt fascination, on a world tearing itself apart.

14. SUPERHUMAN

'Pack your stuff, we're going.'
'What? What you on about?'
'We live somewhere now. We've got a place. C'mon, chop chop.'
'Fuck you *on* about? What place? Where?'
'It's a surprise. Just grab what you can. Essentials. We can come back for other stuff later. And don't forget Ava.'
'I'm not gonna forget *her*, am I?' Where are we even going?'
'You'll see.'
Jane spots Jonny's black eye. 'How did you get the shiner?'
Jonny outlines last night's Cromwellian tear up, sans Barbara Nash references.
Jane shrugs off the account.
Blokes fight.
And?
She goes to find a suitcase. Jonny goes in to chat to her fourteen-year-old brother Danny in his bedroom while he waits. Jonny clocks Porno Tony's *tigers-on-the-mountain* carpet spread across the bed.
'You're not keeping that, by the way.'
'Am.'
Jonny wonders where Jane has put the dildo Nicky threw at him. Somewhere the kids won't see it, hopefully.
Danny is going to be some kind of scientist. Anyone could tell you. Bit of a smart Alec, but Jonny likes him. Danny is animal mad, a nature fanatic. A boy after Jonny's own heart. The natural order of things has always been Jonny's religion, having long ago forsaken his father's maddening adherence to the good book. The room is a shrine to wild birds. The walls are obliterated by large colour photos of kingfishers, hawks and vultures. Books cover every surface.

The antique display case against the wall is crammed with small stuffed birds and collections of tiny eggs stuck on a felt board—tagged and labelled. He shows off his collection to Jonny, who is genuinely intrigued. Jonny pulls a heavy volume from a set of encyclopaedias on the shelf and pushes a pile of American comics off the bed onto the floor to make room for it.

'Bit old for these, ain't cha? The comics?'

'Don't scoff. They're responsible for my fundamental sense of morality.'

'*Fundamental sense of morality*?' Jonny tuts. This kid's precociousness is an endless source of amusement. He glances at the comics at his feet, picks them up, puts them beside him and flicks through a few.

A gimmick.

The Amazing Spider-Man?

No masks for Jonny. *With this face?* Fuck off.

The Incredible Hulk?

Like a muscle-bound Frankenstein. Hasn't got the carriage to carry *that* off.

The *Fantastic Four*?

The stretchy bloke? Old looking.

The brick guy? See The Hulk.

The 'flame on' bloke? Jonny Storm . . . The Human Torch . . . All in blue . . . Blonde hair . . . Turns into a fireball when he yells *'Flame on!'*

Jonny scoops the comics off the floor. 'I'm borrowing these.'

'Help yourself . . . ah!' Danny has found what he's looking for. 'Here it is.'

He pulls out a small glass case containing a grapefruit-sized egg and hands it over.

Jonny lays down the comic and takes the egg. 'So, what came first?'

'That's no chicken egg. That's the egg of an Aquila Heliaca, more commonly known as an Imperial eagle. Very rare, very Spanish.'

'So, what came first? The Imperial eagle or the egg?'

'The egg.'

'The egg?'

'The egg, yeah.'

'That question has annoyed people forever and you know the answer! So, what laid the egg then?'

'Dinosaurs. Dinosaurs were laying eggs 60 million years before birds even existed.'

'Smart arse.'

Connie, having finally vacated the bathroom, comes in and plonks herself down next to Jonny, a large towel wrapped like a turban around her head. These three siblings share Jane's chocolate brown hair and sapphire blue eyes. They could be triplets if not for the years between them. The older one, David, long since left and married with his own kids, is a darker proposition, in nature and in temperament.

Danny tells her, 'Get out.'

'I can come in here if I like, can't I, Jonny?'

'No.'

Danny laughs, accordingly.

'You're horrible to me!' Connie moans, but quickly recovers. 'Why did you marry Jane? Do you love her?'

'I'm gonna marry *you*!' Jonny jests. 'You're my girl, Connie.' He puts his arm around her and makes to kiss her.

'Get off! Get off! Anyway, you can't marry me if you're married already. It's against the law.'

'True,' Jonny says. 'Plus, you're too old.'

Danny pipes up. 'Too stoopid.'

Jonny picks up the big book again. Jane is ready. She stands by the door with a suitcase at her feet, watching him among the youngsters. Jonny sees her watching them. His surprise appearance this afternoon has caught her on the hop. She's had no time to prepare for his arrival. She's somewhat dishevelled—but she looks good—even dishevelled. *Especially* dishevelled. Wormwood's tit-flash comes to him. The kids don't know, obviously, but something tells him to exorcize the memory from his mind in their presence. Today's mission was beyond his control, something that had to be done. But now, the way she stands there . . . a delightful anticipation re-enters the equation.

Living together . . .

Jonny shakes it off and hands the egg back to Danny. 'Come on then, tell us something interesting about birds.'

'Like what?'

'I don't know. Anything.'

'Females only have one ovary?'

'How come?'

'Weight.'

'Can't say the same for your mum. She must have ovaries like Tommy guns.'

'She can't fly neither.'

The boys laugh. Although she doesn't get it, the laughter is contagious, and Connie laughs with them. 'What's an ovary?'

In unison, the boys say, 'Shut up!'

'Oh, you're *horrible* to me!' She marches past Jane and out of the room, sulking.

Jane, a portrait of impatient anticipation, says, 'So what are we doing then?'

'Yeah, hang on . . . Danny, you just reminded me of something. I remember my Mam telling me that when she was a kid, she believed she could fly—absolutely convinced. So, one day in school, she told everyone she was gonna go to this little stone bridge and show everybody that she could fly. Went on about it to everyone all day. So anyway, all the kids followed her down to this bridge, and she climbed up on the ledge, spread her arms out, and in front of all these kids, she leapt and dropped like a fucking brick straight into the stream.'

Danny's laughter is infectious. Jonny and Jane laugh too.

'And the moral is?' Danny splutters.

'No moral. You just reminded me of it, that's all.' Jonny scans the book open on his lap. 'Okay smart arse, what's a gynaecologist?'

Danny considers this. 'Erm . . . Someone who's going 'a' college.'

'You've got an answer for everything, ain't ya?'

Danny mock considers this also. 'Erm . . . No.'

Jonny puts the suitcase in the boot. Jane sits in the back seat with Ava in her basket and the baby bag on her lap.

Jonny switches the ignition and stalls it.

And again . . .

His third attempt catches.

Jane waves to her mother, brother, and sister as they look down from the balcony. The car pulls away and slaloms around the junk, overturned bins and broken glass that litter the road outside the brown brick monolith that is Octavia House.

Jane peers through the back window as her family and previous life diminish into the distance.

All stalling aside—once they got going—Jonny was fine. Those few crash-courses (pardon the pun) from Nicky around the backstreets of Norbury, and those recent A-road runs up north had appreciated admirably.

Jane feeds Ava with a bottle in one hand and runs the other along the door sill. 'How much was this, then?'

'What, the car? A mate's lending it to me.'

'What, that four-eyed berk that dropped you off the other day?'

'Yeah. Nicky. You'll meet him at some point.'

As soon as those words pass his lips, he knows that *that* is never going to happen. Not if Jonny can help it. Especially now with the whole Barbara element dirtying already contaminated waters.

Oh no.

That wouldn't do at all.

Jonny has to wonder: does Nicky know about the Locarno incident? and is he kind of fucking with him?

A loyalty tester?

An inkling, perhaps?

Another one of those little fucking birdies?

Very little happens in Nicky's world that he doesn't know about, so it was inconceivable that the 'all knowing' Nicky Nash can be totally oblivious to his wife's adventures. *And that shit she was on about*—the guy having a heart attack in anticipation of being tortured? What the fuck was *that* about? No question: Barbara Nash was something unprecedented.

But then . . . *nothing'll fuck you quicker than a big mouth, Sammy!'*

The maxim at the root of all criminal endeavour.

Maybe it holds fast.

The very glue that holds Nicky's world together.

Fear and silence are the currency with which the likes of Nicky Nash and Clifford Sherman traded.

But maybe it was a two-edged sword, that silence.

Maybe it created blind spots.

Maybe that's why some people got tortured.

As it would turn out, Jonny would not have to worry about it after all.

Not for a while, at least.

He drives down through ponse country. He looks out for the Cromwellian and expects to see squad cars around it, investigating reports of last night shoot 'em up, up but can see nothing controversial.

Finally, they cross the river into Wandsworth, through Tooting Common until they're cruising along that Capone scar—that A23, Streatham High Road—until they come to a halt on a leafy side street; proper South London.

Jonny has keys and lets them into a three-story house on Brancaster Road.

He carries the basket, urging Jane on up the stairs ahead of him on frayed and tattered carpets, past closed doors on every floor. Silence reigns, and Jane wonders if anyone else even lives here.

On the landing of the third floor, Jonny puts Ava down and fumbles excitedly with the keys, shoulders the door open and, with a theatrical flourish of his open hand, beckons Jane inside.

The room is big and empty but for a queen-sized mattress in the middle of the hardwood floor, piled high with unmade bedding—a small transistor radio next to it. Above them, a shade-less bulb hangs from the baroque coved ceiling.

Jonny steps back out of the room and brings Ava's basket inside and puts her on the floor next to the mattress.

What Jane's assessment lacks in gratitude is more than compensated for in verity. 'What a shit hole.'

Jonny goes to the window, and with difficulty, opens it. 'Yeah, but it's *our* shit hole.'

'You bought this?'

'Rented. From Kareem. One of the wrestlers. We got furniture coming. He owns a furniture place in Stockwell. Gonna give us a discount. Twenty per cent.'

'A cot'd be handy.'

'Behind the door.'

Jane turns and sees the big pink cot against the wall. Half-empty paint tins nearby.

'It was white, so I painted it pink. What do you reckon?'

Jane runs her hand along its freshly coated surface. 'It's sticky.'

'Don't touch it then.'

It was a good job, she has to admit. It has a mattress and two big cuddly toys, a demented-looking clown and a big brown bear with a red silk ribbon around its throat. She scans the room anew and begins to see possibilities. She nods at the unmade mattress. 'Who have you had here then?'

'No one, stupid.'

'No one stupid?'

'Nobody's been here. Silly cow. So, what do you think then? Once everything's in, it's gonna be great.'

'Could do with a wallpapering.'

'We'll get someone in.'

'Fuck that. I'll do it myself.'

'You?'

'Yeah. Why not?'

'Have a go. If it's shit, we'll get someone in.'

'It won't be shit. Any twat can paper a wall.'

She goes to the open window and sees the long-overgrown garden—a neglected lawn flanked by two rows of naked rose bushes; a dilapidated shed full-stopped the area.

She can see it. It could be nice. But the verdict lay with another. She lifts Ava out of her basket, takes her around the room, shows her the garden, and places her in the cot. The baby continues to survey her surroundings with jerky movements of her head then gurgles delightedly. The baby's laughter brightens the room. As if on cue, a cloud moves aside. Warm rays of sunlight caress the dusty floorboards.

They lie mostly naked across the mattress on the floor. He still has his pants around one ankle. Her blouse is open. Her breasts declare themselves with post-pregnancy pride. Her garter belt and bra lie under the sink in the corner.

The faint trill of Ava's snore and the clatter of distant trains are the only sounds to be heard.

Jonny is ready for round three and pulls Jane to him. The room is cold enough to notice. He pulls the covers over them both and loses himself in her again.

Night has fallen. The street lights beyond the back yard offer its orange glow. The room is well and truly christened. Jane contemplates the crawling shadows across the ceiling of the darkening room.

Jonny rests his head on her thighs and traces the shiny tracks of the stretch marks that flank her thighs with languid fascination. Absently, she traces the thick veins of his other hand with a wandering finger. They are roads. Jonny and Jane are at the beginning and at the end of them. Roads of creation.

He knows now that he can do this; the one-woman man shtick. It was contrary to the natural order of things; he knew. But Jonathan Eamon Arnold could master any order, natural or otherwise.

He believed he could tame his beasts.

Therein lay true freedom.

The day's exquisite exertions cried vengeance.

'Wanna eat?'

'Where?'

'I'll go and get something.'

'Now? There's nothing open.'

'There'll be something on the high street. Chip shop, at least.'

Jonny gets dressed, checks on the baby, squeezes her tiny hand, brushes the soft button of her nose and says, 'Won't be long.' and leaves.

She hears the reassuring locking of the front door below. The distant squall of freight trains reminds her of the ones to and from Park Royal at the back of Octavia House. The ones she'd been hearing all her life. Residing in a state of abstraction, her mind wanders. These are different trains now, trains of another world. She slides the volume of the radio to zero before turning it on and re-setting the volume low. Jo Stafford is singing *You Belong to Me*.

You belong to me...

The memory of their pre-birth breakup makes an unwelcome return.
Italy...
Jonny wants the world.
She wants Jonny.
For her, now, this room *is* the world.
She had never imagined herself going anywhere. Not that she could remember. Nor anyone she knew. Even in the war, her dad was in the Home Army. Never went anywhere. Her world was Kensal Rise and surrounding areas which ended somewhere around Portobello Road. And people round there didn't need to go anywhere. The world came to them. There's always been the Italians, the Greeks, the Jews ... and now you had all these blacks coming in. Kensal Rise was no paradise, so how awful must Africa, or wherever they were coming from, be? No. the world came to London. And now she is in Streatham. She thinks about her friends. The ones with motherhood still before them. Inevitable motherhood. What else is there?

You belong to me...

Keys rattle; the front door opens and Jonny comes bounding up the stairs with a large package wrapped in yesterday's newspapers under his arm, a bottle of Coca Cola in one trouser pocket and a carton of milk in the other. The nasal sting of hot vinegar'd fish is wonderful. He checks Ava, who is still asleep, gives Jane the drinks, and opens the package out on the floor. They eat their cod and chips and watch each other eat. Jonny peels away the batter from his cod and puts it put it to one side. Susan Maughan's *Bobby's Girl* comes on the radio. Jane sings along quietly, changing the Bobby to Jonny.

I wanna be ... Jonny's girl ...

He's never heard her sing before. She's good, and tells her so. 'You ever thought about trying to make money out of it, singing?'

'No.'

'Why not?' Jonny gestures with a chip at the radio. 'You're better than that bird.'

'I couldn't get up in front of people. I won a bike once, when I was a kid, but I never got it 'cos I was too shy to get up and get it.'

'What?!'

'It was at Saturday morning pictures. There was a drawing competition, and I won. But when they called out my name, I just froze. Just couldn't get up. When I told my mum later, she nearly killed me. It was red.'

'What was? The bike?'

'Yeah.' Jane swallows another piece of fish. She is right back at that Saturday morning matinee. 'I think about that a lot, that bike.'

'So, what did they do?'

'Who?'

'With the bike?'

'I dunno. Must have gave it to someone else.'

'Pisser.'

Jane finishes her meal and scrunches up the soggy newspaper into a ball. 'So, I don't think you'll see me at the Palladium anytime soon.'

'You weren't so shy that time in the Scrubs.'

'What?'

'The tit flash?'

The memory returns with scarlet cheeks. 'I can't believe I did that.'

The girl is a country he's hardly crossed the borders of. Her cities promise much. 'See. You might surprise yourself yet.' He finishes his food and his ball of newspaper joins hers. 'I didn't tell you, my dad came down to visit.'

'Yeah, you did?'

'Really? When?'

'In the hospital.'

Jonny considers this lost nugget. 'Bet I didn't mention the fight. We were in the middle of a fight when I got the news you were in there.'

'A fight?'

'Yeah. An actual punch up. Silly fucker made a surprise visit for some reason. Probably had a row with Mam. He wanted to stay awhile, which I wasn't too happy about. We went out for the day, but by the time we got back, it all kicked off.'

'What was it about?'

'Can't remember now. Doesn't matter. We've been like that ever since he came home from the war. I wasn't even born when he left. The first thing I remember wanting was my dad, and when he finally came home in '46, he came off the train and hugged everyone. Me last. Probably took him a while to work out who I was. On the ride home, he asked me if I wanted a banana or a Cream Cracker. Bananas were still a rarity. The only time you saw them was on top of Carman Miranda's head at the flickers. But I'd never even heard of a Cream Cracker, and it sounded bloody marvellous. So, imagine my disappointment when he handed me that poxy little dry biscuit. It wouldn't be the last disappointment. Most of our ructions were over going to church on Sunday mornings. I was always adamant that I would never end up down the pit with him, but there was nothing else. So down I went and immediately started making escape plans. By this time, Elvis happened and I realised there was a whole world out there. So escape I did. He only came down to have a nose around, so he could tell everyone back home about how I was wasting my life.'

'Maybe he just wanted to make sure you were okay.'

'That bastard? No. He came to take the piss.'

'Does he still work there? At the pit?'

'Like his dad and his dad before him. The only time he wasn't doing that was when he went in the army and spent three years in a Jap work camp. And *I'm* the loser. I guess he learned a thing or two from them, the fucker.'

Ava wakes up and starts crying. Jane rummages through the baby bag for the nappies. As she changes the baby on the floor, Jonny stands over by the window. The garden jogs troubling memories.

'When I was a kid, I built this hut thing at the end of the garden out of elderberry branches. A critter magnet, I called it. It attracted all kinds of Ebbw Vale wildlife. There was a big frog living in it for a while until it got evicted by a pregnant cat. A grey tabby, it was. It had three kittens, all different colours, so all three of us, my brother and sister, adopted one each. Within days, all the local toms were fighting over the mother, and it went off and left its litter with us. We gave them all names and became their foster parents. Till the old cunt pulled his King Solomon routine and told us that we could only keep one and that I had to decide which. The other two had to be drowned. He kept going on that if I don't choose soon, he'd drown the lot of 'em. I thought it was a joke so took no notice. A fucking wind-up merchant he was. Anyway, I came home from school one day and checked the hut, and they were all gone. He done it. He drowned them all and threw them in the bin.'

Jane holds the cooing baby to her, rocking her gently, while looking at Jonny standing in shadow by the window. For a moment, he seems like a ghost of himself. Like he's faded somehow.

He turns. The shadows somehow shift with him and makes him real again.

'I've never told anyone about that before.'

The tale is horrific. Jonny's unfamiliar openness, even more so. How can a man like this be . . . vulnerable? She feels as if she's falling into some kind of abyss until Jonny—*her* Jonny—returns and comes to the rescue.

'What was the picture of?'

'What picture?'

'The one you drew to win the bike you never got?'

'Johnny Ray.'

Over the next two days, the furniture arrives. Jane will look back on these first few days in their new abode as among their happiest. Isn't it everyone's dream to make a world of their own? And that's what they were doing now; making their life what it should be. Just them. Him, her and the baby. Of course, the big world was out there, but for now, it ceased to be.

On the Friday, he sends her out on an errand. She buys a meter-and-a-half of blue velvet fabric and a Prince Valiant pattern from Pratt's department store. Already, she can picture the result and wonders what the hell Jonny has in mind. On the way back, she finds the chemist on the high street, purchases the final item and returns to find him reading the comic books he borrowed from her brother.

'You get it?'

'Yeah.' She holds up the material and hands over the small box she got from the chemist. 'Got it here.'

He hands her the comic—*The Fantastic Four*. 'This one.' Jonny points at the blue-suited blonde fireball, Johnny Storm. 'I want to look like him.'

He sits with a big plastic napkin around his neck in front of the mirror. His black hair matted down with warm water. Jane stirs the thick pale blue paste around in the porcelain jar with a shaving brush.

'Are you sure about this?'

Jonny glances at the big fur *tigers-on-a-mountain* carpet, hanging on the only wall space big enough to accommodate it.

'Just do it.'

15. WILD WEEKEND

Weston-super-Mare is a seaside town that probably means nothing to you unless you live there, and even less if you do. Tonight, a small crowd gathers around the electrical goods shop. Through the wind and rain of the Bristol Channel, the people are entranced by flickering TV screens in the big display windows of Rediffusion... the television hire place.

'Telly on the never never.'

It's JFK weekend.

Both channels feature the same thing—fresh updates and endless repeats of Jack Ruby's shooting of Lee Harvey Oswald. The news shimmers as the driving rain cascades down the showroom windows.

Everyone *not* crowded around TVs and the radio—and who doesn't feel at least a little sacrilege about being entertained on this earth-shattering weekend—are at the nearby Pavilion, forming an orderly queue around the building. It'll take more than the threat of World War III to keep these people home.

Sunday 24th Nov. Winter Gardens Pavilion,
Weston-super-Mare

KEN "VAMPYRE" WALKER
vs.
JOHN ST. ANGEL

Meanwhile, in London...

It's an after-hours session at the Cromwellian Club. The place is closed out of respect. Plus, it's a Sunday, so fuck it. Only the in-crowd are in attendance: the in-crowd being the four men that constitute "Rich" Clifford Sherman's high-command—an ID line-up of sartorially elegant thuggery.

On the jukebox, The Pentagons are singing *I Wonder If Your Love Will Ever Belong to Me*.

The lounge is illumined by the screen of the television behind the bar and the warm glow of the electric Smirnoff display beside it.

Again, we see the moment of death of the presidential assassin; of Ruby, seemingly punching the T-shirted killer in the guts with his gun.

Enforcer Ray, bouncers Stan and Les and Sherman's right-hand man Sammy Fortnoy are transfixed by the screen as they sit around the bar. Scattered across it are various brands of cigarette packets, half-finished drinks, a half-played game of poker . . . and a Walther Olympia-Pistole .22.

Bouncer Stan exhales harshly on his cigar and waxes prophetic. 'That's it—world war fucking three. If I was in charge, I'd bomb Russia *and* America before we get caught in the crossfire.'

Sammy waxes level-headed. 'Yeah, well . . . maybe that's why you're not in charge.'

Enforcer Raymond says, 'They should be sayin' *save* the fuckin' bomb, not ban it.'

He hears a distant crack. They all do. 'Was that the back door?'

That trapped cloud of nicotine fog swirls languidly above the Pavilion's audience. Seconds and bucket boys busy themselves around the illuminated ring as Geoff the M.C climbs in and untangles the microphone cable from the ropes. His clipped delivery crackles through the inadequate 'not so loud' loudspeakers.

'A-ladies and a-gentlemen! Hammerstone Promotions welcome you to an evening of professional wrestling in the official Lord Mount-Evans style! In the red corner, weighing

in at thirteen stone and ten—from Camberwell, London . . . Ken "Vampyre" Walker!!!'

The "Vampyre", with what little hair he still has, smarmed forward into a black point, steps forward to meet his applause, punches the air a few times, bounces off the ropes and smiles, revealing a big gap where his front teeth should be. He holds out his grey cape, bat-style, and soaks up his reception with all the command and charisma of a second-hand kite. He goes back to his corner, flips off his cape and turns to face his opponent...

There is an ear-piercing crack as the lounge door splinters inwards. All four men cower behind the bar. Nicky Nash steps through the debris with a neatly sewed scar across his left cheek, distorting his customary smirk. He is holding the long ivory-handled Samurai sword that normally lives on his wall.
    Within the tight limitations of his injury, he grins big.
'Howdy.'

In the blue corner, Jonny Arnold is running on the spot. A pristine white hooded dressing gown obscures his visage from the head down. Only his new silver boots are exposed.
    MC Geoff's intro continues . . .

' . . . and in the blue corner, making his Weston-super-Mare debut, weighing in at twelve stone and five . . . from Cardiff, Wales . . . John St. Angel!'

Flinging the gown off dramatically, Jonny leaps forward, revealing a golden peroxide quiff and sideburns. Jane's immaculate powder-blue cape and matching trunks dazzle accordingly. A few silver sequins tie the ensemble together.
    Is he wearing make up?

Jonny had to do something about the black eye he got at the Cromwellian last week. Maybe he went just a bit *too* far with the pancake and eyeliner.

He gives a premature victory sign and bounds around the ring like a muscle-bound albino Elvis. The polite smattering of applause that greets him is drowned out by laughter. This was not on Jonny's litany of expectation. What the fuck is wrong with these people? He is a prince among them now and fucking looks it.

Even the MCs and officials are amused. Jonny took pains to hide his new image from everyone until now. He got ready in the car. You never get a second chance to make a first impression.

But look at his face.

Gutted!

The crowd knows a chink in the armour when they see it and start to prise it open.

A punter yells, *'Blimey, clock the Barnet!'*

Laughter ensues.

Another punter . . . *'Ere, better mind yer arse with that one, Ken!'*

More laughter.

And another jibe, *'Ere, are you some kind of a poof or what?'*

And another, *'Nah, 'e ain't a poof but I bet 'is boyfriend is!'*

Ridicule threatens to engulf Jonny's glory. The laughter is contagious, followed by more barbs of the same calibre as they scramble over their own momentum.

Reg the referee, exuding all due professionalism, with his tight black dickie-bow and patent leather slip-ons, ducks in between the ropes, and calls the fighters into the centre of the ring.

He checks their nails and the toecaps of their boots, each in turn. 'No gauging. No hair pulling and you break when I say break. Go to your corners.'

'This contest will be decided in five six-minute rounds!' MC Geoff testifies. *'Two falls, two submissions or a knockout to decide the winner!'*

Quickly, he leaves the ring and takes his place down at the timekeeper's table.

The bell rings. Jonny is distracted by the still taunting crowd.

The two fighters size each other up and go straight into some bulling arm and neck holds, then a lightning-fast sequence of Full Nelsons, Half Nelsons, and wrists locks—culminating in the Vampyre, manoeuvring Jonny into a Boston crab. Jonny's escape is beautifully executed as he slips out and away from it with little trouble.

Someone issues forth with their verdict.

'*Poof*!'

Les snatches the gun off the bar and aims it at Nicky's face.

Nonplussed is Nicky. 'Is that the Walther I sold Cliff? You will find the mag-release is fucked on it, so I'd put it down if I were you before I stick it right up your arse.'

Sammy tells Les to '*fucking leave it, Les*!'

Stan agrees. 'Les!'

Ray yells, 'Fuckin' shoot 'im!'

Les has never even fired a gun before, let alone shot anyone. And how might a 'fucked mag-release' be a factor? He looks helplessly at the others. Their collective countenance offers nothing. His bottle deserts him and he places the gun back on the bar. Nicky waves him away with the sword, picks up the gun, turns and—BAM!—blasts the jukebox and The Pentagons to Rock-Ola heaven in a raining cascade of splintered glass.

Nicky tut-tuts. 'Mug.'

Ray yells at the shaken bouncer, 'I fuckin' told you to shoot him!'

Jonny is about to launch another attack but is freshly aware of the crowds' unrelenting abuse.

They're getting to him, these fuckers.

Desperation dictates he play up to the homophobia with a cute little skip around the ring. The wind-up backfires as the abuse suddenly soars to a higher pitch. The fight deteriorates into a slanging match between Jonny and the audience, leaving the Vampyre to look on redundantly.

'Poof!'

Panic sets in among the Hammerstone camp ringside. The natives are getting beyond restless.

The Vampyre shouts to the ref. 'What's this prick doing?'

The ref wags a warning finger in Jonny's face. 'Get your fucking arse back in here and fight!'

Jonny gets into it with a woman in the third row. 'You fat bitch, the last time I saw a figure like yours, it had a harpoon sticking out of it!'

The woman is quick. 'The last time I saw a figure like yours, I was sitting on its face!'

The ref escorts Jonny away from the apron and this verbal defeat.

The bout continues.

The jeering continues.

Jonny breaks away from an arm lock and, out of sheer frustration, drop-kicks the Vampyre, connecting all the way. Unconscious Ken sails over the ropes and onto a front row of murderous pensioners, reducing it to a scrambling mess of old coats and liberated false teeth.

The second-row scatters away from the carnage, then surges back to lay siege to the ring. As the realisation spreads throughout the hall, that the Vampyre has been felled by a 'queer,' the place erupts in fury.

'Get the fucking raver!'

A chair is thrown into the ring. And then another. And then a shower of confectionery, stiletto shoes and plastic containers of Ki-Ora orange juice.

Other wrestlers and officials come running out from the dressing rooms at the back of the hall, body-slamming and forearm-smashing their way towards the chaos where Jonny and Hammerstone officials are fighting a losing battle.

The ring is crammed with people punching each other indiscriminately. Others are trampled in the mad scramble to the ring.

Jonny has some bloke by the hair and is using their head to keep his attackers at bay.

Nicky, holding the gun at his side, scoops up a piece of the broken glass from out of the jukebox with the end of the sword and balances it on the flat of the blade. He points the tip at everyone in turn— engaging his fear detector.

He stops at Sammy. Sammy only came onto Sherman's firm after things got iffy with the Krays. To Nicky's mind, this means unsound allegiances. Nicky is not keen on unsound allegiances, so, in a way, the man has made it easy for him.

'Hold your calls, people. I think we have a winner.'

He glides slowly towards Sammy, who backs up until he stops against the wall. The end of the sword finds itself just inside Sammy's mouth. 'Steady.'

Sammy pisses his expensive pants. Sammy splutters 'Nick don't!'

Nicky tips the piece of glass carefully onto Sammy's tongue and takes the sword away, leaving the man's mouth hanging open. Nicky turns away as if to address the others, but turns back super-quick and delivers a sickening uppercut with his free fist.

A bib of crimson immediately ruins Sammy Fortnoy's suit.

A woman outside the ring lunges up at Jonny's groin with her umbrella. She misses her desired target but pierces the flesh of his inner thigh. Blood rolls accordingly.

She lunges again, but Jonny catches it and takes it from her and whacks her directly on the head. The brolly splinters into a thousand pieces and the woman disappears somewhere beneath the ring.

His victory is short-lived. A hearing aid, thrown from the balcony, spins through the air and hits him directly between the eyes. John St. Angel hits the canvas in a blur of peroxide hair and shards of beige plastic.

Sammy is on the floor screaming blue murder, nursing his wrecked mouth.

Les admonishes the bespectacled one. 'Aghhh ... for fuck sake, Nick!'

Stan makes for the hallway phone. 'Let me call an ambulance ...'

'Leave the blower be, Stanley!' Nicky commands. 'Or I'll cut your hand off!' Stan relents. Without looking around, Nicky senses Ray's movement. 'Don't you fucking move, Ray!'

Whatever Ray had in mind is cancelled.

Satisfied the room is his, Nicky plays comic-depression and huffs big. 'Where's Clifford?'

'He's not here', Les says. 'He's gone to see Harriet at the Golden Guitar.'

'And when might one expect him?'

'Anytime now.'

Satisfied, Nicky takes a stool at the bar, places the sword and gun upon it and pours himself a large, neat Johnny Walker.

Sammy is on his knees by the wall, catching falling gore from his mouth.

Nicky gulps his drink, shudders and says, 'Stanley, take him to the shitter, will ya? He's giving me an 'eadache! Les. Ray. Sit down.'

The two men pull up stools at the other end of the bar as Stanley manoeuvres a whimpering Sammy Fortnoy to the toilets.

The commotion on the television attracts Nicky's attention. 'What's this?'

Les tells him. 'They've shot the bloke that shot Kennedy.'

The BBC repeats the death scene yet again. Some weedy non-entity in a white t-shirt is led out through a door into a crowd by a bunch of cowboy cops. Someone in the crowd lunges forward.

BAM!

Video distortion rolls the scene until the image rights itself. The weedy non-entity hits the deck. Somehow, the non-entity attains significance.

The flickering screen absorbs Nicky's complete attention.

Or does it? Les and Ray exchange anxious glances and weigh up their chances.

Too late.

Nicky snaps out of it. 'You know what you're looking at, doncha? Ten years' time, all they'll have on television is executions . . . murders.' Nicky nods to the screen. 'That's the future, that is.'

The hallway door clatters.

'What happened to the fucking door?' The lock's broke—'

'Rich' Clifford Sherman, in all his Gieves & Hawkes finery, swans into the lounge holding the broken lock, sees Nicky sitting there and stumbles back, aghast.

'Ah,' Nicky says, 'speaking of executions . . .'

Sherman throws the lock. 'Nicky! No!' The lock misses Nicky by a mile and smashes the mirror behind the bar.

Nicky snatches the Walther off the bar, slides off the stool, steadies the gun over his forearm—Bond-style—and BAM! puts one straight through Clifford Sherman's right ear. His criminal mind shatters the door he came in through with a sloppy smack.

The rest of him slumps to the carpet like dumped laundry.

To the best of anyone's recollection, Weston-super-Mare has never seen a riot: certainly not a full-scale 'un.

Inside the Pavilion, chairs sail through the air.

A corner of the ring collapses. An avalanche of wrestlers, ring rats and punters spill out across the ballroom floor.

Out on the street, debris rains down indiscriminately. Chaos for chaos' sake.

Squads of Black Mariah vans pull in tight around all the Pavilion's exits.

The law exacts instant justice with fists, boots and truncheons.

Actual justice is a thing of the morning.

In Hull, a crowd of teenage girls are screaming at The Beatles.

In Washington DC, the murdered president lies in state. His killer's body is being prepped and autopsied in Dallas.

The 1960s have just caught up with all of us.

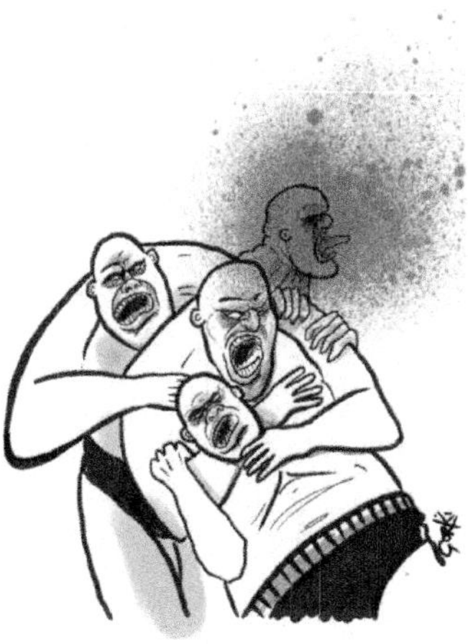

ACKNOWLEDGEMENTS

To my father: the main inspiration for this book. Thanks for the stories, Pops.

And thank you, Colin MacInnes, Ted Lewis, Harold Pinter, Jez Butterworth and Alan Silitoe for putting the wiggle in my literary stride. (One hopes)

Also, mucho gratitude to my test readers Shirley Jones, Mike Dalton and 'Southside' Jimmy Price. Once again, I owe you copies.

For the true stories behind this work of fiction, check out the 'Exotic' Adrian Street autobiographic series.

My Pink Gas Mask
I Only Laugh When it Hurts
So Many Ways to Hurt You
Sadist in Sequins
Imagine What I Could Do to You
Violence is Golden
Merchant of Menace

Available from Amazon

Next up...

The World Belongs to Jane & Me – Part #2: 1968

Also from A. D. Stranik: the debut novel,
Monomania, Mon Amour.

"A fate worse that death. A crime worse than murder!"

Praise for Monomania, Mon Amour...

Amazon reviews

☆☆☆☆☆ "A gonzo pilgrimage into the soul of the modern mythos."
☆☆☆☆☆ "Written in Panavision. Great book!"
☆☆☆☆☆ "Divinely dark!"
☆☆☆☆☆ "Compelling, brutal and Exciting!"
☆☆☆☆☆ "Definitely the raunchiest book I've ever read!"
☆☆☆☆☆ "Sin-sational!"
☆☆☆☆☆ "An absolute fireball of a book!"
☆☆☆☆☆ "Excellent debut!"
☆☆☆☆☆ "Superbly written, dark and visceral."
☆☆☆☆☆ "A cross between Dash Hammett and Hunter S. Thompson."
☆☆☆☆☆ "Smart, zappy and full of character!!!"
☆☆☆☆☆ "Revel in the wonderful murky madness that blew my mind!"
☆☆☆☆☆ "If you enjoy the darker side of fiction, look no further!"
☆☆☆☆☆ "Sexy, raw and bloody. Gives Tarantino a run for his money.
☆☆☆☆☆ "I devoured it in a few days, just couldn't put it down."

"Stranik is a powerful wordsmith who is, despite this being his debut novel, already making an impact in the literary world."

(Inside Time)

ABOUT THE AUTHOR

Adrian David Stranik is a musician from South West London.
His father was a wrestler.
His mother made many of his father's iconic outfits.
He lived in Milton Keynes.
He spent a lot of time in America's Deep South.
He now lives in Bedford, England.
The World Belongs to Jane & Me - Part#1: 1963 is his second book.
He doesn't own any animals.

(Photo by Ben Chamberlin)

Printed in Great Britain
by Amazon